THE
WINTER
Duchess

A Duchess for All Seasons
Book One

JILLIAN EATON

This is a work of fiction. Names, characters, places and incidents are either the product of the author's imagination or are used fictitiously, and any resemblance to actual persons, living or dead, business establishments, events, or locales is entirely coincidental.

© 2017 by Jillian Eaton
ISBN: 9781973353287

www.jillianeaton.com

"HAVE YOU EVER BEEN KISSED, CAROLINE?"

"K-k-kissed?" she sputtered.

"Yes. Kissed." He took one step towards her, then two, and before she quite knew what was happening he'd sat down on the edge of tub and had his hand in the water, fingers trailing through the bubbles in an absent circle that was creeping dangerously close to her thigh.

"I – I don't know." Is the water getting hotter, she thought frantically, or is it just my imagination? Suddenly she felt less like a lady enjoying a calm, relaxing bath and more like a boiled lobster. One about to be devoured by a very hungry duke.

"You don't know?" he said, amused. "I should hope you would remember. Perhaps it wasn't done properly."

"Perhaps not," she said faintly.

"I've always found the prelude to a kiss to be the most important part. You need to not only make your intentions known, but to set the mood." His eyes, as dark as a stormy sky, slowly traveled over every inch of her wet, quivering body before they settled on her flushed countenance. His mouth curved. "Don't you agree?"

"What – what are you doing?" she demanded when he rested his forearm on the curved edge of the tub and leaned in close enough for her to smell the muskiness of his cologne, a combination of leather and brandy.

"Setting the mood," he murmured....

CHAPTER ONE

As CAROLINE STOOD BESIDE the man she was about to marry, she wasn't thinking about him. She was thinking about her mother. Specifically, what her mother would do if her only daughter suddenly turned on her heel and bolted out of the church.

She wouldn't scream. Lady Patricia Wentworth *never* raised her voice. But she would no doubt deliver The Look, which was a thousand times worse than a screaming tirade, and Caroline – being the good, dutiful daughter that she was – would meekly return to the altar to pledge herself to a stranger she knew positively nothing about…except that she was terrified of him.

Unfortunately, she was also afraid of her mother. And if she had to choose between the devil she knew and the devil she didn't, she would rather choose the one who – so far, at least – hadn't given her any sorts of looks aside from mild disdain.

While the priest read a passage from *The Book of Common Prayer*, Caroline dared to sneak a quick glance at her husband-to-be. Her pale lashes flicked up and then down, skimming across the top of her cheeks upon which the smallest spattering of freckles rested.

Her mother had tried all sorts of remedies to get rid of the freckles, from lemon juice to a ginger paste that had stung horribly, but the small brown dots had been stubbornly resilient. For the wedding she'd dusted Caroline's entire face with a powder that had made her sneeze repeatedly, much to Lady Wentworth's general annoyance.

"Stop that," she had said with exasperation, her long, skeletal fingers wrapping around the jutting bones of her hips as she'd met her daughter's watery gaze in the dressing mirror. "You cannot sneeze your way through your vows! Just imagine What People Would Say."

Lady Wentworth had always been exceedingly concerned with What People Would Say. Caroline was never quite sure what people she was referring to, but whoever they were they must have been very important.

"Perhaps we can postpone the ceremony?" she had asked hopefully. "If we wait until spring-"

"Do not be absurd. We are not postponing anything. Now hold still, these curling tongs are hot."

As she peeked at her husband-to-be, Caroline couldn't help but wonder if he had powder on *his* face. She sincerely doubted it. He didn't seem at all like the sort who would have something as common as freckles.

The Duke of Readington stood still and straight as a statue with his face turned slightly away, giving her a clear view of his profile. Eric was, if not a handsome man in the traditional sense, a very distinctive one with bold, slashing brows set above clear blue eyes that made her think of a frozen lake in the middle of winter. His nose was long and straight. His rigid jaw impeccably clean shaven. In fact, everything about him was rather impeccable from the sable locks swept back from his temple and set in place with a bit of pomade to the fold of his cravat and the lines of his black tailcoat. He must have had an excellent valet.

And a very brave one, Caroline thought silently. Every one of her encounters with the duke thus far had been fraught with tension and anxiety. She could not imagine the nerve it must have taken to attend to him on a daily basis.

As if he could sense she was thinking about him,

his head swiveled and she found herself the unwilling recipient of his glacial stare.

He said not a word. He did not have to. The hard set of his mouth and the line between his brows spoke volumes. With a tiny squeak she directed her gaze forward, hands trembling ever-so-slightly as she adjusted her grip on the bouquet of white lilies her mother had thrust upon her before she'd entered the church.

For Caroline, the rest of the ceremony passed by in a bit of a fog. When the priest asked her to recite her vows she did so automatically; her lips and tongue forming the words that would bind her to the veritable stranger standing beside her until death did they part even as her mind remained detached, as if she were observing herself from a great distance.

She woke from her daze when the duke reached for her hand. She instinctively pulled back, her entire body leaning away from him like a sailboat caught in a stiff westerly wind. He frowned, those cold blue eyes of his narrowing to icy slivers of disapproval, and with a deep breath she forced herself to give up her limb. After all, what was one small hand when she was surrendering her entire body?

The gold band he held poised at the tip of her left ring finger was very plain, making her wonder if it was a family heirloom. Had it belonged to his mother? Had she stood right here, in this very church, and recited the very same vows? Had she been frightened? Or elated? When it was over had she cried tears of happiness? Or wept with sorrow?

Caroline was distracted from her thoughts when Eric began to speak, his deep voice resonating from one end of the church to the other. He stared not at her, nor into her, but *through* her, as if she were as translucent as the gossamer coverlet draped over the front of the altar.

"With this ring I thee wed."

Oh dear, she thought weakly. *This is it.*

"With my body I thee worship."

You've really stepped in it this time, Caro.

"And with all my worldly goods I thee endow.

Well that bit doesn't sound too *terrible.*

"In the Name of the Father," he continued solemnly, "and of the Son, and of the Holy Ghost. Amen."

A shiver raced down Caroline's spine when he slowly slid the ring on to her finger, pushing it all the way back until it touched her third knuckle. It was a bit too large, which was fitting, as everything about this marriage felt a bit too large from the man holding her hand in a grip so tight it was almost painful to the title she now wore like a yoke around her neck.

In only a matter of minutes she had gone from Lady Caroline Danvers, daughter of a simple earl, to the Duchess of Readington, wife to one of the most powerful men in all of England. It felt so surreal that had her fingers not ached from the force of the duke's grip she might have thought she was in a dream.

"You are hurting me," she whispered.

He glanced down at their joined hands and immediately loosened his grip, but did not offer an apology, nor did she expect one. Her fingers tingled as blood rushed back into her hand and she was so distracted by the sensation that she did not realize the ceremony had ended until her new husband stepped down off the dais and held up his arm.

Like a doll whose appendages were being expertly manipulated by a child, she walked with careful precision down the aisle, taking two small steps for every one of the duke's larger ones. No one clapped as they passed between the pews, but a few did incline their heads in a gesture of respect. Not towards her, of course. She was no one. A failed debutante plucked from the shadows of obscurity for reasons she'd yet to fully understand. But they did respect her husband. Or, perhaps more accurately, they feared him.

There were more people waiting for them outside of the church. Men and women dressed in their Sunday best, all hoping to catch a glimpse of the duke and his new duchess.

"Smile and wave," Eric ordered between clenched teeth. "You look like a frightened field mouse."

Caroline *felt* like a frightened field mouse. One that had just fallen into the jaws of a surly, ill-tempered cat who hadn't yet decided if he wanted to play with her or eat her in one satisfying gulp. But she was nothing in not obedient, and so she lifted her arm and swayed it back and forth in a motion that, if not *exactly* a wave, was close enough to satisfy the duke.

Women and children threw rice and flower petals at them as they descended into the crowd. Taking hold of her elbow, Eric steered her towards the gleaming black landau that would ferry them away to her new home.

The team of matching grays stood quietly while she mounted the steps and climbed inside. Struggling with the train of her dress she gave it a hard yank and nearly tumbled top over teakettle onto the floor. The duke caught her before she could fall, his withering stare telling her precisely what he thought of her clumsiness.

"Sit over there," he said, pointing to the opposite

seat, "and make yourself comfortable. It is going to be a two hour journey."

"So long?" she whispered, paling at the thought of being trapped alone in a carriage with her husband for more than two minutes, let alone two hours.

"Speak up," Eric said irritably. "I cannot understand you when you mumble like that. Didn't your governess teach you how to properly enunciate?"

Her governess had, in fact, taught her how to enunciate. An adept student with a quick mind and a thirst for knowledge, Caroline could enunciate in five different languages. What her governess *had* failed to teach her was how to deal with a monster for a husband.

If Eric had shown her even an ounce of compassion or understanding she might have been able to keep her tears at bay. She was, by nature, a sensitive woman, but she'd never been an overly dramatic one. She usually reserved her tears for her pillow, but as the reality of her new life began to sink in there was no holding them back any longer.

"Are you – are you *crying*?" he asked incredulously, dark brows sweeping up towards the sharp brim of his hat when she let out a soft, sad little sniffle.

"No," she lied miserably.

His eyes narrowed. "It certainly appears as though you are."

"I – I'm not."

Sniffle. Sniffle.

"Stop it at once," he commanded, as though tears were something that could be turned off as easily as a leaky tap or a faulty spigot.

"I am trying." And she was. Truly. But unlike her husband, she could not hide her emotions behind an icy façade of indifference. When she was happy she smiled. When she found something amusing she laughed. And when she was miserable and tired and frightened, she cried. Grabbing for her reticule, she pulled out a white handkerchief and tried to dry her cheeks, but for every tear that she managed to whisk away two more fell.

The duke's sigh of exasperation filled the carriage. "Well at least turn your head so I do not have to look at you."

Crumpling her handkerchief into a tiny damp ball, Caroline sniffled and looked out the window. For a little while everything was blurry, but when she finally stopped crying she found herself gazing at gently rolling fields that stretched as far as the eye could see. Fluffy white sheep dozed in the sun, soaking up what was left of a summer that had all but reached its end, and the sight of the contented livestock brought a tremulous smile to her lips despite the heaviness in her heart.

She had always loved animals. Unfortunately, Lady Wentworth despised anything with fur. Or quills or feathers, for that matter. She'd tried countless times to convince her mother to allow her just one single pet. Even a goldfish would have sufficed. But the answer had always been a firm and unyielding no.

"Who do they belong to?" she asked softly, watching as a lamb jumped to its feet and went bouncing across the field. It must have been born late to have still been so very small, and she hoped it would be brought into the barn before winter struck. Without a thick coat for protection the poor little dear would surely freeze to death in the snow and the ice.

"To what are you referring?" Eric said brusquely without bothering to glance up from the newspaper he'd unfolded across his lap. Since entering the carriage he had loosened his cravat and removed his hat, but the informal state of his attire did little to dull his hard edges.

"The – the sheep." Caroline bit her bottom lip. She hated the nervous tightness that arose in her belly every time she spoke to the duke, and could only hope the uncomfortable sensation would fade with time. After all, she couldn't be afraid of her husband *forever*.

Could she?

"They're mine." The newspaper rustled softly as he turned to the next page. "We entered Litchfield Park while you were blubbering into your hanky. All of these fields, and the animals within them, belong to me. If you have any further questions you may direct them to the butler, Mr. Newgate, when we reach the estate." And with that he returned to reading, leaving Caroline to stare at him in stunned disbelief.

She had known the duke was wealthy. But she'd had no idea he owned hundreds - no, hundreds of *thousands* - of acres. And this was only *one* of his estates! Rumor had it there were at least four more, along with two houses in Grosvenor Square, a hunting lodge in Scotland, and a collection of private residences scattered throughout Europe. The magnitude of it all was overwhelming, to say the least. How could she possibly be expected to manage one household, let alone dozens? Surely there had been some mistake. She wasn't supposed to be here, sitting across from one of the most powerful men in all of England. And yet here she was.

Giving a small, bemused shake of her head,

Caroline turned back to the window. As the countryside continued to roll past she contented herself by counting the sheep and it wasn't long before she fell into an exhausted, dreamless slumber.

CHAPTER TWO

ERIC CHARLES EDMUND HARGRAVE, sixth Duke of Readington and Earl of Baylor (among other less significant titles), watched his new bride sleeping with a clenched jaw and narrowed eyes. He'd suspected the journey was not going to be a pleasant one, but had he known she was going to start bawling before they'd even left the churchyard he would have demanded she travel in her own coach.

Having grown up with a manipulative mother who had constantly used her tears to bring his father to heel, he could not abide crying in any form. A fact his last mistress, a beautiful widow with a penchant for naughty antics between the sheets, had learned the hard way.

Eric felt no guilt for ending the seven-month arrangement. He had been more than generous to Melody during their time together, and he'd settled a handsome sum on her when they parted ways. Truth be told he'd quite enjoyed her. Out of all of his mistresses, she had been one of his favorites. But when she'd begun pressing for more than he was willing to give - and dissolving into tears like a petulant child when he refused her demands - he knew the relationship had run its course.

Fortunately, the Melody's of the world were quite easy to replace. Once he'd settled a few matters at Litchfield Park he would return to London and find another mistress. Preferably one who wasn't so bloody dramatic.

Eric's dark brow furrowed as he continued to stare at his sleeping bride. One of the matters he needed to resolve before departing was the matter of an heir. At nine and twenty he was beginning to feel the pressure that plagued all titled men when they began to reach a certain age without having yet procured a son.

His pressure was intensified all the more by his dissolute scoundrel of a younger brother. A brother who stood to inherit - and lose - everything he had spent most of his adult life rebuilding after the late Duke of Readington bled the Hargrave fortune dry at the gambling hells. It had taken him nearly a decade to regain what his father had lost, and he'd be damned if he allowed all of his hard work to go to naught.

The money did not mean anything to him. Money could be lost and gained and lost again. But the land -

the land where his ancestors had lived and died for nearly three hundred years - meant something. And he refused to let the estates, specifically Litchfield Park, go to someone who did not understand their significance. Which was where Caroline came in.

With her pink lips slightly parted and a loose tendril of white blonde hair clinging to the curve of her cheek, she looked like a sleeping angel. It was the first time he had ever seen her at peace. Whenever he'd happened to glance upon her countenance before now she'd always appeared frightened, as if she were one second away from jumping into the nearest broom closet.

She was a meek little thing he mused, rubbing his chin. Not that he minded. One of the reasons he'd selected her was *because* of her shyness and timidity. He certainly hadn't picked her to be his bride because he desired her. A snort bubbled in the back of his throat at the very idea. Caroline was one of the least desirable women he had ever encountered. Which was precisely why she was going to be such an excellent wife.

When a man wanted passion, he found himself a mistress. When he wanted a rightful heir, he found himself a wife. And only a very foolish, very stupid man ever attempted to have both with the same woman.

The late Duke of Readington had been such a man and he'd paid a dear price for his stupidity. A dear, dear price. One that had made him the laughingstock of the entire *ton* and had ushered him into an early grave.

Having seen firsthand the pain and the heartache that unrequited love could cause, Eric had no intention of repeating his father's mistakes. Once he was assured Caroline was carrying his child, he would be returning to London with all haste. She, of course, would remain at Litchfield. If the mood struck he would return time to time to see how she and the babe were faring. Or, at the very least, send a proxy in his place. After all, he wasn't a *complete* monster. Just a very matter-of-fact one who knew precisely what he wanted.

And it wasn't love.

Caroline began to stir as the carriage left the main road and started up the long, winding drive that led to a sprawling country house built of white washed stone. It was not the largest estate in his possession, nor even the grandest, but the thirty-seven room manor and its surrounding fields and meadows would be more than sufficient for one woman and her child.

His shy new bride would want for absolutely

nothing at Litchfield Park. If she desired a pink flamingo it would be brought to her with a gold ribbon tied around its skinny neck. But his generosity did not come without certain stipulations.

"You're awake," he said when she lifted her head and blinked drowsily at him. "Good. Before we disembark, I should like to take the opportunity to make a few things clear." She blinked again, and he could tell the moment she became acutely aware of her surroundings because her gaze suddenly dropped to her lap and her slender shoulders caved inwards beneath her dark gray cloak as if she were a tiny bird seeking shelter from an impending storm.

Eric gritted his teeth. He'd wanted a wife who wouldn't dare challenge him, not one so frightened of her own shadow that she quivered with fear whenever he tried to *talk* to her. It wasn't as if he had yelled at the girl or raised his hand in anger. Yet she was terrified of him just the same.

What had he called her at the church? A frightened field mouse? Yes, that was it. Although looking at her now he wasn't reminded of a rodent, but rather of a fawn. A shy, spindly legged fawn with soft gray eyes framed by thick lashes and a full bottom lip that trembled ever-so-slightly when she peeked up at him before quickly glancing back down.

Absently he wondered what that quivering mouth would taste like. Soft and sweet, he imagined. Like the sugar sprinkled on top of a biscuit or a bit of honey drizzled into a cup of warm tea...

Eric scowled, annoyed that he'd allowed his thoughts to drift in such a fanciful direction. Kissing his wife was not something to be looked upon with great anticipation. It was a responsibility. A duty. A task he would carry out not because he *wanted* to, but because he *had* to if he wanted to keep his brother from destroying everything he'd so painstakingly rebuilt.

"Have I done something to upset you?" Caroline whispered, her cheeks draining of what little color remained as she noted the heavy furrow in his brow. "Because I've stopped crying-"

"You've done nothing," he said shortly. "But perhaps we should have this discussion at a later date. When you've had time to settle in to your new surroundings and rest."

They drew to a halt at the end of the circular drive and the door was promptly opened by a young footman neatly attired in black livery. He stood at attention with his gaze politely averted while Eric stepped out of the carriage and then turned back to reach for Caroline's hand.

Enclosed in white lace, her fingers were as small and delicate as the rest of her and stood out in sharp contrast against the deep black of his coat sleeve. He felt her tremble as she lifted her head and looked up at her new home with wide, unblinking eyes, taking everything in from the solarium comprised entirely of glass to the outdoor terraces that wrapped around the third and fourth stories. There was even a tower jutting up from the east wing. It had been closed off years ago, but was still an impressive sight to behold with its stained glass windows and circular roof.

"Litchfield Park was part of my mother's dowry," he explained in the flat, mildly disgusted monotone he always used whenever he spoke of the woman who had given birth to him. "It was completely renovated just last year. You should be very comfortable here."

"It's enormous," Caroline said softly.

He shrugged. "It is not nearly as large as Readington Crossing, but I believe it will be more than suitable for raising children." He saw no point in telling her that the *real* reason she was here was because of the estate's remote location. Tucked away in the middle of the Surrey countryside, it was a four day ride to Readington and another two to London, effectively ensuring his wife would not be bothering him with any surprise visits.

"The stables are that way-" lifting his arm, he pointed off to the left where a stretch of white fence line was just visible through a row of towering shrubbery "-and the orchards and greenhouses are behind the house. There is more, of course, but Mr. Newgate will be able to give you a full tour."

"Couldn't you do it?" she asked, tearing her gaze away from the tower to peer up at him out of soft gray eyes brimming with uncertainty and just a touch of wistful hope. Her grip on his forearm tightened and Eric frowned when he felt his loins stir in response to such a small, innocent touch.

"Couldn't I do what?" he said suspiciously. When had her eyes gotten a hint of green in them? And why the bloody hell was he looking at her mouth again and imagining what her lips would taste like? A trick of the light, he decided, and a touch of exhaustion. God only knew he hadn't slept much the night before.

Thoughts of his impending marriage had kept him tossing between the sheets well into the cold, dark hours of early morning. When he'd finally risen it had been with the grim determination that no matter what came, he would not repeat the sins of his father. He would not give his wife control of his heart and stand idly by while she gleefully tore it to shreds. He would not become a broken shell of his former self, spending money like water and drinking himself into oblivion.

And he would not, under any circumstances, fall in love.

"Give me a tour of the grounds. I - I just think," she added hastily when his brow creased, "it would behoove us to spend more - more time together now that we are married. Don't...don't you agree?"

"No," he said flatly. "I do not agree. In fact, I could not *disagree* more strongly."

The corners of her mouth tightened in distress. "But-"

"Mr. Newgate will show you to your private quarters. I have more important things to attend." With that icy remark he turned on his heel and strode briskly away, the heels of his boots stomping the ground with so much force that small stones flew up in his wake.

CHAPTER THREE

CAROLINE WATCHED HER HUSBAND walk away with an aching in her chest that bordered on despair.

He hates me, she thought bleakly. *He hates me and I haven't the faintest idea why.*

Perhaps she'd said something that had upset him. But that would have required them to have had a conversation lasting more than a few sentences, which they'd yet to do. Maybe she'd done something he had found untoward...but then again, she'd spent more time having her face powdered than in the duke's company.

A cold wind, hinting at weather yet to come, had Caroline pulling her cloak more snugly around her shoulders. The carriage pulled away, leaving her standing alone in the middle of the drive without any idea of what to do next. She was supposed to be a duchess...but Eric had dropped her on his doorstep as if she were an unwanted relation and then gone - well, she had no idea *where* he'd gone because she knew absolutely nothing about him. Or this place; this large, overwhelming, foreign place that she was now supposed to call home.

This time when tears threatened she managed to sniff them back. She wasn't about to give the duke an excuse to despise her any more than he already did, nor did she want to step off on the wrong foot with the household staff.

Unlike many of her peers, Caroline's gentle nature had always lent itself to a relationship of kindness and respect between herself and the working class. She wanted the same at Litchfield Park, especially since it seemed as though the servants were going to be the only ones speaking to her. She had no friends here. No family. As for her husband...well, suffice it to say he should have been both but instead he was neither. For the first time in her life she was completely and utterly alone.

"Might I offer you some assistance, Your Grace?" This came from the footman who had opened the door when they'd first arrived. Wrapped up in her own melancholy thoughts, Caroline had completely forgotten he was standing no less than three feet away.

"Oh!" she gasped, flattening a hand across the top

of her chest. "I - I am terribly sorry. I just...I don't know what...that is to say...oh drats," she said helplessly when her eyes flooded with tears. What was *wrong* with her? Surely being left in front of the house as though she were some sort of vagabond orphan was enough humiliation for one day. She didn't need to add sobbing in front of a footman to the list.

"Your Grace?" the young man repeated, looking vaguely alarmed.

"I - I do apologize," Caroline managed between sniffles. "I'm not usually like this, you see. But then things are not at all like they usually are, are they?" She pulled off one of her gloves and used it to dry her eyes. "Could you be so kind as to direct me to Mr. Newgate? I believe he is supposed to give me a tour."

"Of course, Your Grace. Right this way." Looking relieved to be passing her on to someone else, the footman led her up between two enormous ivory pillars and into the grandest foyer she'd ever seen.

The first thing that caught her eye was the gold chandelier hanging down from a vaulted ceiling, its dozens of candles reflecting off the marble tile beneath. A grand staircase rose from the middle of the foyer and led up to a double hallway that was so long it stretched out of sight. The air carried a hint of beeswax, no doubt from all of the mahogany trim that gleamed from a recent polish.

It was a splendid entryway. One that truly befitted a duke.

But not his duchess, Caroline thought silently as she peeked into the adjoining parlor. There was a heavy masculine overtone to everything, from the deep green paper hangings to the leather furniture. There was also a sterileness to it all. A cold formality that made her wonder if her husband had ever spent any time here. Without a single personal memento - not even a painting - the dark, somber house could have belonged to anyone.

A door to her right opened and an older man stepped through, his chest swelled with self-importance and his knobby shoulders proudly erect. He wore the black suit and the white lapels of a servant of high importance, leading Caroline to guess she was about to meet the estimable Mr. Newgate even before he strode up to her - perhaps hobbled would have been a better word - and bowed.

"Your Grace," he said in a raspy baritone that aged him just as much as his gray hair and the myriad of lines upon his weathered countenance. "It is a pleasure to finally meet you. I am Mr. Newgate, and I have served as butler for the past thirty-seven years."

"That is quite an impressive feat, Mr. Newgate." She hesitated. "My husband asked that you show me around the estate. If it isn't too much trouble, that is. I know you must be very busy and I would not want to take up your valuable time..."

"It would be my pleasure, Your Grace. Shall we start with the library?"

"Yes," Caroline said, her face brightening. "That would be splendid. Oh, and Mr. Newgate, if I could make one small request. I realize that I am a duchess now and that it carries its own title, but I really would be much more comfortable if you and the rest of the household staff called me by my given name. You could even shorten it to Caro if you like."

The butler looked positively scandalized. "Certainly not, Your Grace," he huffed. "Certainly not. If you would allow Thomas to take your cloak and gloves, we shall begin in the east wing with the library and work our way westward. Follow me, if you please."

Well it had been worth a try. Handing her outer garments off to the footman, Caroline smoothed her hair, shook a wrinkle from her dress, and followed the butler.

AFTER HER TOUR - which consisted of all thirty seven

rooms excluding her husband's private study and bedchamber - Caroline found herself quite exhausted. She was shown to her room by a plain-faced servant named Anne who, after learning that Caroline had not brought her own lady's maid, eagerly volunteered herself for the position.

"I've never been one before," she confessed, brown eyes anxious and hopeful. "But only because there's never been a lady at Litchfield Park before. Well, at least not while *I've* been here. But I'll do whatever you require of me, Your Grace. I like to work. And I'm quite handy with a pair of curling tongs."

Caroline sat on the edge of the canopied bed. "What do you know about removing freckles?"

"Re-removing freckles, Your Grace?" Anne bit her lip. "Not very much, I am afraid."

"Then in that case I believe you will make a splendid lady's maid." A genuine smile - the very first one in what felt like a very long while - flitted across her face when Anne let out a squeal of excitement.

"Oh, *thank you*, Your Grace!" she cried, all but bouncing up and down. "Thank you! I will not let you down. I promise. Where should I start? Would you like me to put away your things?"

Over the past hour carriages bearing trunks filled to the brim with Caroline's various dresses and accessories had begun arriving. After four failed seasons she'd managed to accrue more than her fair share of ball gowns, and it seemed her mother - who had taken it upon herself to do all of the packing - hadn't wanted to leave a single one behind.

"Or draw you a bath?" Anne continued enthusiastically. "Or fluff your pillows? Or take down your hair? Or-"

"If you would be so kind as to close the curtains," Caroline interrupted, "I believe I shall take a rest. Could you wake me before dinner? I would like very much to dine with my husband."

"Oh. But...of course, Your Grace."

"Is something about my request unusual?" she queried, noting the way Anne's gaze flitted suddenly to the side.

"N-no," the maid said haltingly.

"I fear you are about as good at telling a fib as I am, Anne." Her mouth curved. "Which is to say not very good at all. What is it?"

Visibly squirming, the hugged one arm tightly against her side and shifted her weight from foot to foot. "It's just that...well...it isn't a love match, is it?" she blurted. "You and the duke. I thought...that is to say, everyone knows…"

"That my husband hates me," Caroline said softly when Anne trailed off.

"No, Your Grace! That isn't what I meant-"

"The curtains, if you would." Suddenly feeling very weary indeed, she pushed herself towards the head of the bed and drew a soft wool blanket up over her waist. "Please close the curtains."

CHAPTER FOUR

WHEN CAROLINE AWOKE, dawn was just beginning to unfurl ribbons of light across a clear blue sky and a small fire crackled cheerfully in the hearth. For a moment she laid where she was, her gaze drawn to the silk damask canopy draped over the top of the bed. She hadn't meant to sleep the entire rest of the day and night away, but she was glad that she had as she felt, if not completely free of the cumbersome weight that sat atop her shoulders, at least a tiny bit refreshed.

Sitting upright, she drew the wool blanket around her shoulders as a shiver worked its way down her spine. For all their size and splendor large houses were quite drafty, and despite the fire there was an unwelcome chill in the air that would only grow colder as the weeks progressed and the bright colors of fall gave way to the brittle starkness of winter.

Of Anne there was no sign, but the maid must have

been in the room at some point for draped over the back of a wooden rocking chair Caroline found a day dress along with a neatly folded petticoat and a satin-trimmed corset.

With a start she realized that she'd slept in her wedding gown and the pale blue frock, once so painstakingly starched and pressed, was now wrinkled beyond repair. Not only that, but three pearls had worked their way free of the stitching on the bodice and were now missing. After several minutes spent searching for them amidst the sheets, she gave up with a sigh and rang for Anne.

The maid appeared almost immediately. Wearing a high necked black dress, white apron, and a worried frown, she hurried through the door and nearly stumbled over her own feet when she threw herself forward into a deep curtsy.

"Your Grace, I wanted to apologize for what I said yesterday. It wasn't my place. My mum is always telling me I run my mouth too much. Anne, she says, you're bound to get tossed out on your ear one of these days." She lifted her head, revealing fretful brown eyes beneath a creased brow. "Oh, please don't sack me. I won't say another word about you and the duke. I swear I won't."

"I am not going to sack you," Caroline said firmly.

"You - you're not?"

"No. I do not believe anyone should ever be punished for speaking their mind." She tucked a loose curl behind her ear. "Does...does everyone believe what you told me yesterday? That my husband and I...that is to say…"

"You did not marry for love?" Anne ventured.

"Yes." Relieved the maid had been able to say what she could not, Caroline nodded vigorously. "Precisely."

It may have seemed foolish - and it probably was - but when she was a young girl she had not dreamt of fancy gowns or glittering diamond tiaras or balls that lasted all through the night. Instead she'd dreamed about finding her true love. A man who was kind and handsome and made her laugh. He needn't be wealthy or own a great mansion or even be titled. Just as long as he gave her a reason to smile every day. Of course her mother had had other ideas, and what Lady Wentworth wanted Lady Wentworth got - even if it was at the expense of her own daughter's happiness.

Caroline could have always refused the duke's suit when he made his intentions known, but that would have meant not only defying one of the most powerful men in all of England but also her mother...who, although not as physically imposing, was every bit as intimidating.

So she'd done what they had both wanted her to do. She'd married a man she hardly knew and traveled to an estate she knew not at all. A frightening undertaking to be sure, but in the back of her mind she had retained some sliver of hope that her new husband, while grouchy as an old bear on the outside, was really a kind, affable man beneath all the sullenness and glowering stares and curt remarks.

That hope had been dashed from the instant they'd arrived at Litchfield Park. And to make matters worse - because no matter how bad things appeared, they could *always* get worse - it seemed she had been the only one who had thought there was ever a chance she and Eric might one day come to care for one another as a husband and wife should.

Apparently love was not a very realistic expectation when a surly duke was involved.

"I don't know how to answer your question," said Anne, chewing on her lip.

"Honestly, if you would," Caroline said before she marched across the room and pulled back the drapes. Small fractured crystals of ice still clung to the outside of the windows, but they quickly melted into droplets of water when her breath warmed the glass. Resting her hands on the sill, she gazed out across rolling fields painted silver with frost. It was a pretty sight; one made all the prettier by a herd of frolicking horses. Emboldened by the crisp morning air they bucked and danced their way across the pasture, their hooves scarcely touching the ground.

"The duke has never been a very...warm man," Anne began hesitantly. "When the staff learned of his engagement, it was assumed the marriage was...well, that it was an arranged one. But from what I understand that is not uncommon, Your Grace."

"No," Caroline said softly, still looking out the window. "It is not uncommon at all."

But it still did not make the sting of being trapped in a loveless union hurt any less.

Why, she wondered silently as she watched an energetic bay prance and snort and toss his head. *Why choose me, of all people?* But that was one question Anne could not answer, and she dared not ask it of her husband. At least not yet.

"Could you help me undress?" Feigning a bright smile, she turned around and lifted her hair to the top of her head, exposing a row of pearl buttons running down the length of her spine. "I fear I cannot do it myself."

"Of course, Your Grace." Looking relieved to have been given a task that did not require her to divulge any more personal information about her employer, Anne helped Caroline out of her wedding gown and into the yellow dress she'd laid out on the chair.

Simple in design, it hugged Caroline's shoulders and small breasts before falling away from her hips in a swirl of muslin and ivory lace. It was supposed to be worn with a hoop skirt, but she had always found the large, cumbersome contraptions dreadfully uncomfortable. She could not wait until they fell out of fashion, along with the boned corset that made it nearly impossible to draw a deep breath. Whoever invented the confining undergarments, it certainly hadn't been a woman.

Not wanting to put Anne through the trouble of drawing a bath, she washed her face and arms with rose scented water and then sat perfectly still while the maid brushed out her hair before twisting it into a simple coiffure that left gold ringlets dangling down on either side of her temple.

"Don't you want a feather or two?" Anne asked. "Or perhaps a flower?"

Caroline shuddered. Had her mother been in attendance she would have refused to let her leave the room without a full stone's worth of accessories weighing down her head. Why, just two months ago she'd been forced to cut a *bird's nest* out of her hair -

complete with eggs! - after her lady's maid had used a bit too much hemp-wool and powder to secure it.

"No." The word felt heavy and foreign on her lips. Not surprising, given she wasn't accustomed to speaking it. With her mother hovering over her shoulder she'd spent the last twenty-one years being told what to wear, what to say, and what to do. But now Lady Wentworth wasn't here...and if she didn't want flowers or feathers or bird nests in her hair she didn't have to have them.

"That will be all, Anne. Thank you very much for your assistance." She met the maid's gaze in the looking glass and smiled. "You are going to be a wonderful lady's maid."

Anne blushed. "Is there anything else I can do for you?"

"I believe I'll stretch my legs before taking breakfast. Do you happen to know where my fur-lined cloak is? It should have been in one of the trunks, but I haven't any idea which one. My mother was rather overzealous in her packing," she said apologetically.

"Not to worry, Your Grace. I will have it brought to you right away."

"Thank you, Anne. I'll be waiting in the foyer. Oh, and Anne?" she asked before the maid could hurry out the door. "I do have one more small request."

"Yes, Your Grace?"

"Please…call me Caro. You needn't do it in the presence of Mr. Newgate," she said hurriedly when Anne frowned. "I know he wouldn't approve and I do not want you to get in any trouble on my account. But when we are alone, just the two of us, I want you to think of me as your friend." Her mouth curved in a tremulous smile. "I could very much use a friend."

"You know," Anne said thoughtfully, "you're not at all like I thought a duchess would be."

Caroline's smile faded. "I'm not?"

Oh dear.

One day in and she was already mucking it up. She'd known being a duchess wouldn't be *easy* and despite all of her lessons in etiquette and manners she had suspected there would be bumps and blunders along the way.

She just hadn't realized she'd had time to make any yet.

"No. I always imagined a duchess to be…well…" – the maid's hand waved vaguely in the air – "hoity-toity and full of airs. But you're really quite nice."

Caroline blinked. Out of all the things she'd been afraid of doing wrong, being too nice had never occurred to her. She sat up a bit straighter in her chair.

"Thank you, Anne. That…that is very kind of you to say."

"You're welcome." The two women exchanged smiles and then with a quick curtsy Anne left the room, leaving Caroline to wonder if perhaps her new life wasn't going to be quite so terrible after all.

ERIC PULLED HIS STALLION up short when he saw a cloaked figure standing beside the horse pasture, their arm extended between the wooden rails as they reached out to touch one of his prized thoroughbred broodmares.

An equestrian enthusiast from the moment he'd sat on his first pony, the duke's carefully cultivated breeding herd was one of the finest in all of England. The foals his mares produced were worth tens of thousands of pounds and just this spring one of his two-year-olds had taken the Derbyshire Cup, the youngest to ever do so.

To say he was protective of his horses – particularly his broodmares – would have been a vast understatement. No one except for himself and his grooms were ever allowed to touch them. They weren't pleasure animals, they were breeding stock. And they – bloody hell. Was that a *carrot*?

"You there!" he called out sharply. "Step back at once!"

Ignoring him, the cloaked figure climbed up on the fence and stretched their arm all the way through the rails, an orange carrot dangling from their fingertips as they tried to coax Lady Rebecca, the dam of the colt who had taken the Derbyshire Cup, a few steps closer.

Gritting his teeth, Eric pressed his heels into his stallion's sides and the great black thoroughbred leaped forward as though springing from the starting gate. As they came thundering down over the crest of the hill the interloper panicked and squeezed himself between the rails, tumbling headfirst into the pasture.

"Got you now," Eric said grimly, but no sooner had the words left his mouth than the rest of the mares, enticed by the smell of a stallion, came running across the field in a rippling wave of sleek muscle and deadly hooves.

He was of half a mind to let the stupid fool get trampled to death. It would be no less than he deserved for trying touch one of his horses. But then the stupid fool's cloak fell back, revealing soft yellow hair spun from gold and the terrified countenance of his wife. Lurching to her feet, Caroline ran towards the fence and jumped onto the middle rail, clinging to it like a kitten dangling down from a tree as the herd of mares came barreling towards her.

"God*dammit*," Eric cursed as the anger in his chest turned to ice. Pulling hard on the reins, he leapt from the saddle before his mount had come to a full halt and sprinted towards the fence. Grabbing hold of his wife's slender forearms, he yanked her up and over the top rail just as the mares reached them.

Clods of dirt and grass rained down from the sky as they fell backwards. Instinctively protecting Caroline with his own body, Eric struck the ground first. Grunting from the force of the impact, he rolled once, twice, and came to a stop in the shade of a towering oak tree with Caroline cradled on top of his chest.

She was so still that for a moment he feared she'd been knocked unconscious...but then he saw a flash of gray as she peeked down at him through her tangled hair and his fear turned to fury.

"You little idiot!" he growled, blue eyes flashing with temper. "You could have been run down! What the devil were you thinking, climbing into that field? Those horses are easily ten times your size!"

"I – I am sorry," she whispered haltingly. "I was only trying to–"

"Get yourself killed?" Eric gritted his teeth as he

fought the urge to shake some sense into her. He'd known his wife was cripplingly shy, but he hadn't any idea she was so dimwitted! Or so soft…

When she tried to push herself upright her hip brushed against his upper thigh and he suddenly found himself gritting his teeth for another reason all together.

It wasn't because he found her attractive. She was pretty enough in a wallflower sort of way, but his personal preferences had always run towards more exotic beauties. Ones with dark hair and full red lips and heated glances that could burn a man from across the room. Caroline had none of those traits, and yet as she squirmed and wiggled he could feel heat shooting straight to his loins.

"Stop that," he said harshly.

She looked down at him in confusion. "Stop what? I am not doing anything."

He groaned when her breasts brushed against his arm. "Stop *moving*. Unless you want our son to be conceived underneath a tree."

"No – no," she squeaked.

"Good." Jaw clenched, he waited for his arousal to pass. But when it didn't – when it only got worse – he propped himself on his elbows and glowered at the bewitching blonde sprawled on top of his hard, pulsating body. "I need you to stand up."

Caroline bit her bottom lip, and the sight of her plump mouth caught between her teeth was nearly his undoing. "But you just said–"

"I know what I bloody well said!"

What the devil was *wrong* with him? He could feel his heart racing the same as it had when he'd been an inexperienced lad of sixteen about to divine the pleasures of a woman's flesh for the very first time.

Two months without a mistress and I am lusting after my own wife, he thought in disgust.

Who did he think he was?

His father?

The unsettling thought was just what Eric needed to bring him to his senses. Wrapping his hands around Caroline's waist, he set her off to the side before springing to his feet. Brushing leaves off his fawn colored breeches, he stiffly extended his right arm down towards his wife but with a hurtful glance she gathered her skirts and managed to rise without his assistance.

"What is it?" he said on an exasperated sigh when she continued to look at him like a lost little fawn peering out through the bushes at a big hungry wolf. "You're not going to start crying again, are you?"

Even though she did look suspiciously close to

tears, Caroline gave a tiny, albeit firm shake of her head. "No. I just wanted to say – I wanted to say that you needn't yell at me all of the time." She lifted her chin, revealing a spark of defiance he had never seen before. "I've done nothing wrong."

"Nothing wrong?" he said incredulously. "You nearly got yourself killed!"

"I did not know the horses would come running so quickly."

"You never should have been near their field in the first place, let alone inside of it." He scowled down at her. "My horses are prized possessions, not pets. You're not to go near them again. Do you understand?"

"I wasn't going to hurt them," she whispered, looking so dismayed that Eric was nearly tempted to pull her back into his arms.

His brow furrowed. What was it about his tiny slip of a wife that made him think such foolishly romantic thoughts? His mistresses had been after him for years to show emotion. *'It is like you do not care for me at all'* they'd say, to which he always pointed out – quite reasonably – that he'd showered them in a small fortune's worth of furs and jewels. What else could they possibly want? They'd known what they were agreeing to when they had climbed into his bed. And not a single one of them had ever been able to make him feel any guilt for his callousness.

Except for Caroline.

"I know you weren't," he said gruffly. "I should have told you that the fields were off limits." His fingers wrapped around the nape of his neck and sank down into the corded muscle. "Do you like to ride?"

To his surprise, she nodded. Given how tentative and easily frightened she was, he would never have taken her for an equestrian. It took a certain amount of boldness to climb atop a twelve-hundred-pound animal. No horse was completely infallible, not even a sweet-tempered gelding, and every time a person placed their foot in the stirrup they were putting themselves at considerable risk for injury.

"That's something we have in common, then." His mouth stretched in what he thought to be an encouraging smile, but Caroline did not look very convinced.

"I suppose." She nudged a clump of grass with the toe of her boot. "Would you – would you care to go riding together sometime?"

"I don't see why not," he said.

Visibly startled, she looked up at him with wide eyes. "Do you really mean that?"

"I do." As much as he would have liked to, he

couldn't ignore her *completely*. She was his wife, after all. And if they were going to spend time together, he'd rather they do it in the saddle. "I have a colt who could use the exercise, and an older draft mare that would make a fine lady's mount."

"That sounds lovely," she said, and her small, tentative smile aroused a flicker of warmth within his cold, unfeeling heart. Not liking the sensation, nor what it implied, he took a step back both figuratively and literally.

"Very well. I shall bid you good day, then."

"You – you're leaving?"

"I have other things to do," he said brusquely.

"What sort of things?" she called after him when he started to walk away.

He stopped short, a cutting retort souring the tip of his tongue, but when he looked back at Caroline the only sound to come from his lips was a startled hiss of air.

Bloody hell. Had he really thought her a plain wallflower? Standing beneath the red and orange leaves of the oak with her hair unbound and her skin kissed by sunlight she looked like a woodland fairy princess. One plucked straight from the pages of a Shakespearean play.

There was an etherealness to her beauty that he'd

never noticed before. An understated elegance that glowed from within her. She was a quiet sunset after a long summer's day. She was the soothing moment of calm after a hard storm. She was fresh snowfall on an open field. And in that moment he wanted her so badly that he ached.

"Your Grace?" she said uncertainly, making Eric realize that he'd been staring at her with his jaw agape like some sort of love struck fool.

"What?" he snapped, hands diving into his pockets as he rocked back on his heels. "What the bloody hell do you want now?"

Caroline started to say something. Stopped. Frowned. "Nothing." She spoke so quietly that Eric thought he'd misheard her until she added, "I want absolutely nothing from you."

And for the very first time since they'd met, *she* walked away from *him.*

CHAPTER FIVE

THE MAN IS AN ABSOLUTE BEAST, Caroline thought as she stalked across the lawn, blinking furiously against the tears that stung the corners of her eyes. *And it's no wonder he asked me to marry him. Why, I bet no one else was brainless enough to have him!*

Marrying a duke was every debutante's dream come true. But *not* when the duke in question was an arrogant cad who cared more about his horses than his own wife! Maybe he should have left her to be trampled. At least then she would not have to deal with his general insufferableness.

Dashing her handkerchief against her cheeks where a few tears had managed to escape, she stopped short and forced herself to draw a deep breath. No matter what her husband said – or did – she refused to become the sort of wife who burst into tears at every little provocation. Contrary to what Eric, she was *not* prone to dramatic airs.

If she was going to find some semblance of happiness in her new life then she needed to start by working on her own backbone. Maybe then her husband's insults, instead of stinging like nettles, would merely slide right off her back like water from a duck.

What had he called her in the church? *A field mouse*, she recalled with a frown. Well, perhaps it was time she stopped being a mouse and started being a cat.

She was given a chance to test her claws the next evening when she stumbled across Eric reading in the library. Her first instinct was to mumble an apology and duck right back out again, but instead she forced herself to square her shoulders and select a thin volume of poetry from one of the shelves.

"What are you reading?" she asked as she sat down next to him in an oversized leather chair that dwarfed her small frame. It was so large that her feet did not even touch the bearskin rug laid out in front of the fireplace and after several moments of trying to make herself comfortable she finally gave up and tucked one slender leg underneath her hip. It certainly was not the most ladylike of positions, but it wasn't as if her husband was looking at her, so what did it matter?

"A book," he grunted without so much as a glance in her direction. Firelight bathed one side of his face in a warm orange glow, illuminating the rigid line of his jaw and the firm set of his mouth. His brows were drawn together as he read, his gaze intent on the page before him. He might as well have been wearing a sign round his neck that said 'Do Not Speak to Me'. Unfortunately for him – and for her – that was precisely what she intended on doing.

You're a cat, she reminded herself. *Not a mouse that is going to run scurrying under the nearest sofa at the first sign of trouble.*

Setting aside the volume of poems she had been pretending to read, she took a deep, bracing breath. And then, before her newfound courage had time to desert her, she blurted the one question that had been plaguing her since they'd exchanged their vows in the church.

"Why did you marry me?"

"What do you mean?" he asked without bothering to look up.

Caroline blinked. "I – I thought I was rather clear."

For a moment the only sound was the merry crackling of the fire, and then came Eric's heavy sigh. "Do you really wish to discuss this right now?" he said, dragging his gaze away from his book with obvious reluctance. "Or can it wait until morning?"

She gripped the armrests so tightly that her nails made small crescent indentations in the buttery soft leather. "I – I suppose it could wait, but I would rather discuss it–"

"Very well." He snapped the book closed with so much force that she jumped. "I married you because I needed a wife. There. Does that answer your question?"

She blinked again. "Well…no. No, I am afraid that doesn't answer it at all. Why – why did you pick *me* in particular? There were a hundred, mayhap even a *thousand* other women who were more eligible to be a duchess."

"A thousand may be overstating things a bit. Did you see the latest crop of debutantes?" Eric shuddered. "The one poor girl's face was so long she would have fit right in with my horses."

She frowned. "That's a very cruel thing to say."

"It's not cruel, it's the truth," he corrected. "And the truth is rarely kind."

"Be that as it may, I believe you understand what I am trying to say. We were strangers when you proposed."

"I don't know if I would have called us strangers," he said, rubbing a hand across his jaw where a day's worth of stubble had grown.

"We had only danced once. You called me Catherine when you asked me to be your wife." The embarrassing memory still caused her cheeks to flush. "I believe that is the very definition of strangers."

"I did not call you Catherine." His brow furrowed. "Did I?"

"You did," she confirmed. "You got down on one knee and took my hand and said, 'Dear Catherine, will you do me the honor of being my wife'?"

"Hmm." One shoulder lifted in a careless shrug. "I suppose I did, then. And what did you say?"

Caroline stared at him in disbelief. "I said yes, of course! Why else would I be here?"

"Ah," he said, the faint tracing of a smile lifting one corner of his mouth. "But *why* did you say yes? You yourself just admitted we were strangers. I didn't even know your name. Why would you ever accept such a proposal?"

Why indeed?

"Because – because I felt obligated, I suppose. One does not say no to a duke."

"No, one does not," he agreed. "And there you have it. The reason why I married you."

"I…I am afraid I do not understand."

"To be quite blunt, I need an heir. You see, my

brother is the rather unscrupulous sort. Were he to inherit the ducal title I fear he would squander the estates and drain the coffers in a fortnight. Quicker if he could manage it. But in order to produce an heir, I need–"

"A wife," Caroline whispered.

"Precisely," he said with a nod, looking pleased that she'd finally caught on.

"But that…that still does not answer my original question. Was there something you saw in me?" she asked hopefully. "Something that drew you to me?"

He thought about it for a moment. "Well, I do like blondes."

"Blondes," she echoed hollowly.

"Indeed. Although I've nothing against brunettes. Or redheads, come to think of it. My first mistress was a redhead. Lovely woman." His eyes narrowed. "And she never asked questions. Of course, I did not marry you *just* because of your hair color."

She breathed a sigh of relief. "Oh, thank goodness. You see I rather hoped, with time, that we might come to care for–"

"I needed a young, obedient, malleable lady from good breeding stock. You fit the bill quite nicely on all accounts."

Malleable?

Is that how he saw her? Something to be twisted and kneaded and formed into whatever shape he wished? Caroline felt the color drain from her cheeks as she untucked her leg from beneath her hip and stood up. Her foot tingled from being bent at an unnatural angle for so long but she ignored the uncomfortable sensation, too incensed by her husband's words to even notice the pain.

"That – that is a horrible reason to marry someone!" she sputtered.

"Really?" Eric drawled, a hint of amusement glinting in his cool blue gaze. "Pray tell, what do *you* think is a good reason for marriage?"

"Friendship. Affection. Understanding." She was tempted to say love, but her newfound courage only extended so far.

"Interesting," he said softly. "Should I tell you why *I* think people marry?"

"Actually, I really do not–"

"Convenience. Nothing more and nothing less than the convenience of being with someone who can give you what you want. I want an heir. You want wealth and social standing. No need to make it more complicated than it has to be." He stood up. "This conversation has lost its appeal. I bid you goodnight." Something flickered in his gaze as he glanced down at her. Something that made the tiny hairs on the back of her neck tingle. Something almost…*possessive*. A trick of the light, she told herself. Eric wasn't possessive of her. Truth be told he didn't even seem to *like* her all that much.

She waited until he'd left to sink back down into the leather chair and draw both knees to her chin. It was clear now that she had made a horrible mistake by marrying the duke. She should have refused his suit when he first approached her, but she had been so dazzled at the prospect of being courted by one of the most powerful men in all of England that she had never considered what the repercussions might be.

I should have known it was too good to be true, she thought bitterly as she gazed into the smoldering fire. He hadn't chosen to court her because he fancied her or found her witty or charming. He'd courted her because he thought she was weak and easily controlled. And she was. As much as it pained her to admit it, she *was* weak and malleable and obedient. She always had been.

But that did not mean she always had to be.

"I'll show him," she told the empty room. "Just wait and see."

CHAPTER SIX

WHILE CAROLINE'S INTENTIONS were good, she had failed to consider how uncooperative her husband was. For the next seven days, whether by incident or design, he avoided her at all costs. When she walked into the library he walked out. When she went outside he slipped back in. When she was upstairs he was down. Before long they were no more than two ships passing in the middle of the night, which was why she was so surprised when he appeared in the solarium one morning while she was eating breakfast.

Comprised almost entirely of windows, the solarium offered a beautiful view of the stables and surrounding pastures. It was the closest she had dared get to the horses since she'd almost been trampled to death, and she loved watching them frolic and play while she had her breakfast.

"Your Grace," she exclaimed, setting her cup of

coffee down with a clatter when the duke's broad shouldered frame filled the doorway. He was dressed for the outdoors in a navy blue waistcoat, gray breeches, riding boots, and gloves. "I – I was not expecting you."

"That much is obvious," he said, the corners of his mouth tightening with ill-disguised annoyance when his gaze swept from her blonde hair, pulled lightly back from her temples and secured with two jeweled pins, down to her walking dress. For a moment those cold blue eyes lingered on the swell of her breasts before they jerked back up to her face and his frown deepened into a scowl. "You're not even ready."

"Ready for what?" she asked cautiously.

"Our ride."

Caroline blinked. "I was not aware we had one scheduled."

"If you do not want to go–"

"I do." She sprang to her feet, nearly upending her coffee in her haste to push back her chair.

After nearly two weeks spent confined to the grounds, a ride through the countryside sounded positively heavenly. It would also give her the opportunity she'd been waiting for to show her husband just how *un*obedient she could be. Maybe then he would look at her with longing instead of loathing…and their marriage of convenience would turn into something so much more. "I'll just need to change into my riding habit."

Eric inclined his head. "I will be in the foyer."

With Anne's assistance it only took a few minutes for Caroline to don her riding habit. Comprised of a fitted jacket with long sleeves that tapered at the wrists and a bustled skirt, the burgundy habit was expertly tailored to her slender frame. She finished the outfit with a ruffled cravat and a black velvet hat that sat low on her brow. Turning a quick circle in front of the dressing mirror to ensure nothing was amiss, she smiled nervously at Anne.

"How do I look?"

"Splendid," said the maid, clapping her hands together. "Absolutely splendid. The duke's not going to be able to take his eyes off of you."

Caroline liked the idea of Eric being unable to look away from her. Not that it was likely to happen. If he found her desirable even the tiniest bit, he'd yet to show it.

After their conversation in the library where he'd revealed the only thing he wanted from her was an heir, she'd laid awake at night staring out the window, her muscles tight with anticipation as she awaited the sound of a soft knock upon her door.

When it never came – not that night, nor the next four – she began falling asleep as soon as her head hit the pillow, too weary to wait up for a husband who apparently had no interest in making love to his wife.

The irony was that she actually *wanted* to kiss the duke. Even though he'd been nothing but rude to her, at one and twenty it was high time she kissed someone. And Eric did seem like the obvious choice, given they were married.

"You'd best hurry," Anne said with a pointed glance at the door. "His Grace doesn't like to be kept waiting."

Thanking the maid for her help, Caroline picked up the heavy hem of her skirt and hurried downstairs. She found Eric precisely where he had said he would be: standing in the middle of the foyer, hands clasped behind his back, a look of marked impatience upon his countenance.

"Finally," he snapped when he saw her. "I've been waiting for nearly an hour."

"It has been ten minutes," Caroline snapped right back without thinking. Her eyes widened. "Er…that is to say…it has been ten minutes, Your *Grace*."

His eyes narrowed. "You look different. Have you cut your hair?"

"My hair?" Unconsciously her hand drifted to the

nape of her neck where Anne had fashioned a twisted bun. "No."

"Have you lost weight?"

Her hand fell down to her waist. "I do not believe so."

"Well *something* about you is different."

At a loss, Caroline was helpless to do anything but shrug. "I don't know what it could be. I haven't changed anything."

"Perhaps it's your dress." His gaze flitted down the length of her body before returning abruptly to her face. "It's too tight."

"Too *tight*?"

"Yes. Much too tight. How are you going to ride?"

Experimenting, she lifted her arms and twisted side to side. "It doesn't *feel* too constrictive. I think it is merely the style of the habit."

He crossed his arms and scowled at her. "Well I don't like it."

"I shall make sure to pass your critique on to the dressmaker."

"Are you *mocking* me?" he demanded.

"Of course not," she said solemnly even as she crossed two fingers together behind her back. "Would you like me to put on something else?"

He continued to look at her suspiciously, as if he

knew she was having a bit of fun at his expense but he could not determine how. For her part Caroline kept a straight face even though she felt very much like smiling. She had no idea what had come over her, but for once she did not feel anxious or tongue-tied or any of the other countless nervous conditions that always seemed to afflict her whenever she was in the company of her husband.

"No," he said at last. "We haven't the time."

A footman opened the door and they walked out to a grassy circle in the middle of the stone drive where two horses were already tacked and waiting.

"This is Buttercup." Eric gestured to a palomino mare with a sweet, docile expression. "She's a bit slow, but she's steady. You shouldn't have any problems with her."

Caroline thought it was a bit presumptions of him to assume what kind of rider she was before he'd ever seen her on a horse, but she merely smiled and took the reins from the groom. "We're going to be great friends, aren't we?" she told Buttercup before stepping up on the mounting block and swinging herself gracefully into the saddle.

Like all saddles constructed for women, it had a fixed head and a leaping head, the latter of which enabled her to ride with both legs on the same side of the horse. The seat itself was flat and offered less stability than a man's saddle which was slightly curved at the cantle, but then Caroline had learned long ago that things were often more difficult for the fairer sex.

They just did not complain.

"Where are we going?" she asked brightly once her husband had climbed atop his mount – a tall, gangly looking bay colt with a sliver of white running down the middle of his face – and gathered the reins.

"Follow behind me," Eric said curtly. "And do try to keep pace."

With that he pressed his heels into the colt's sides and the two took off at a brisk trot down the tree-lined drive, leaving Caroline and Buttercup standing in a swirl of stone dust.

"Come on old girl," Caroline whispered, giving the mare's sturdy neck a brisk pat. "We'll show them, won't we?" The draft seemed to bob her head in agreement and moved gamely out when Caroline gave her a light kick.

They followed the duke and his energetic colt across the road and into a barren field. Recently harvested, it was waiting for the soil to be turned over so it could rest during the winter months and give life to new crops in the spring. Large black crows stood guard over what little remained, their beady eyes keeping a close watch on Buttercup as the mare hopped over a discarded pile of cornstalks.

"Well done," Caroline exclaimed, and draft gave a proud toss of her head. For such a large horse she was impressively light on her feet and even though Eric and his colt were ahead of them, it wasn't by very much.

Enjoying the sting of the cold autumn air against her cheeks, she urged Buttercup into a rocking canter. The draft's plate-sized hooves drummed against the partially frozen ground as they loped across the field, sending crows scattering left and right. Laughing with sheer delight, Caroline pulled the mare up shy of a stone wall and rewarded her with another pat and a leisurely walk on a long rein. Having ridden ahead, Eric circled back when he realized his wife was no longer behind him.

"She likes you," he said, nodding towards Buttercup as he pulled his colt alongside the draft. "The last lady to ride her could barely manage to get a trot out of the old gal. Well done."

It was the first praise he had ever given her, and Caroline blushed.

"Thank you," she said shyly, stealing a glance at him from beneath the slanted brim of her hat. His dark hair had been pushed back by the wind and he'd rolled his sleeves up, revealing the corded muscles in his forearms. A sheen of perspiration marred his brow, and more sweat glistened at the top of his chest where he'd unbuttoned his shirt. As she stared at him Caroline felt an unfamiliar warmth steal across her body. It began in the bottom of her belly and quickly spread all the way up to her breasts. They tingled in response and her blush intensified when she felt her nipples swell and harden.

Good heavens. She hoped she was not falling sick. The last time she'd felt this hot and achy she'd succumbed to a fever that had put her on bedrest for the better part of a month.

She looked away from her husband and instantly felt better…until he reached across Buttercup's withers and touched her wrist, his thumb resting just above her pulse.

"What – what are you doing?" she asked warily, regarding his hand as one might a particularly venomous snake. His fingers were long and elegant, his nails short and expertly filed. She really needed to meet his valet and pay him her compliments. The man was truly excellent at his job. Of course, it did not hurt that he had been given such a fine specimen to work with. Eric could have been turned out in a brown paper sack and he still would have looked like a Greek God.

"Your gloves. They are nearly worn through." He turned her wrist to reveal a row of loose stitching. "Why did you not say you needed new ones?"

"Because I do not." She snatched her hand away. "My gloves may be worn, but they are perfectly suitable."

Her husband lifted a brow. "There's a hole in the right one."

"Maybe that is the way I prefer them." Caroline did not know why she was being argumentative, especially over such a mundane matter as gloves. Perhaps because she felt picked apart, like a painting that wasn't quite up to snuff. First he'd thought her hair too short, then her waist too thin, then her dress too tight…and now he had a problem with her *hand wear*?

"You are not even wearing gloves," she pointed out.

"I prefer to ride without them."

"Well I prefer to ride with gloves that are broken in."

He leaned back in his saddle. "Those aren't broken in. They're simply broken. I've also noticed your dresses are a little…shall we say…out of season. I'll have a tailor come tomorrow to take measurements."

"My dresses are–"

"Let me guess," he interrupted. "Perfectly suitable? They may have been suitable for the daughter of a – what title did you father hold?"

"An earl!" Caroline said, piqued that he couldn't remember.

"That's right, an earl. But you're a duchess now. The standards are higher. As my wife, you'll be expected to set the fashion trends. Not come stumbling along three years behind them."

There was a smile lurking around the edges of his mouth, making her wonder if he even knew how insulting he was being. Probably not. The man was too obtuse to consider anyone else's emotions. Especially those of his wife.

"If you hate everything about me then why did you marry me?" Snatching up Buttercup's reins, she kicked the mare into a canter without bothering to wait for a reply.

IF YOU HATE EVERYTHING about me then why did you marry me?

Caroline's parting words echoed in Eric's mind as he watched her ride away. Here he'd thought they had been having a witty exchange, but apparently she'd taken his criticisms to heart. His brow furrowed. Maybe he shouldn't have said that part about stumbling along three years behind, but devil take it he didn't know *what* to say to her! Or any other lady, for that matter. His interactions with women had almost always taken place in one of two places, the ballroom or the bedroom.

In the ballroom he'd gotten away with polite observations of the weather. As for the bedroom…well, he'd never spoken very much at all. And what he *had* said would never be the sort of thing a man could repeat to his wife. Which left him floundering about like a fish tossed up on shore.

Hate?

He didn't hate Caroline. He was rather beginning to like her…and therein laid the problem.

He wasn't supposed to *like* his wife. He wasn't supposed to feel anything for her at all except for mild disdain, and in the church that was precisely what he'd felt. Mild disdain tempered with a sense of obligation to do his duty and produce an heir. But they weren't in the church anymore…and with every day that passed his attraction towards her was growing whether he wanted it to or not.

Ever since he'd seen her standing underneath that blasted tree he'd been unable to get her silky golden hair out of his mind. Or the soft curves of her body. Or the pink softness of her lips. There was no way around it. No way to unsee it. The woman was a bloody vision. A gray-eyed siren sitting high on a rock, singing her sweet song of temptation while sailors crashed their boats at her feet. And his vessel was heading straight towards her…in more ways than one.

When she'd descended the staircase this morning, looking all prim and proper in her ruby red riding habit that hugged every decadent line of her body, he'd been tempted to sling her over his shoulder and carry her right back up the stairs. But he hadn't. He hadn't because he feared once he tasted her sweet mouth he would only crave her all the more.

Or maybe not. Maybe once he bedded her this unwanted need clawing away at his insides would go away once and for all. Then he could focus on more important matters, like returning to London and finding a mistress.

Yes. That's what he would do. It's what he *should* have done the very first night they were married. Wed and bed, wasn't that the old saying? No doubt made up by men eager to return to the fields of battle. Because taking an axe to the neck was preferable to living under the same roof as one's wife for longer than a fortnight.

His mind made up, Eric spurred his mount into a gallop.

CHAPTER SEVEN

"WHAT ARE YOU DOING?" Her fork pausing in midair, Caroline stared at her husband with ill-disguised shock as he walked into the dining room and sat down across from her.

"What does it look like I am doing?" Ignoring the maid who was hastily putting together another setting, Eric rested his elbows on the edge of the table and leaned towards her. He'd exchanged his breeches for trousers and his waistcoat for a formal black jacket complete with cravat. Aside from a single errant curl that hung low over his brow, his dark hair was slicked back and his face was clean shaven, giving her a clear view of his distinguished jawline. "I am having dinner."

Not wanting to risk staining the front of her dress with lamb soaked in a thick butter cream sauce, Caroline slowly lowered her hand. "But – but we never dine together."

"Well tonight we are." He unfolded his napkin and draped it over his lap. "How is the lamb? Cook always tends to make it a little dry."

"It – it's fine." After their ride this morning Eric had disappeared without a word and she'd spent the rest of the day practicing her needlework and playing solitaire in the drawing room.

At precisely half past six she'd gone up to her bedchamber to retrieve a book of poetry before returning downstairs for dinner where she'd planned on doing what she did every night: reading by candlelight while enjoying a superbly cooked meal and then retiring to the parlor for a glass of sherry before bed.

It was a routine she'd established after it became readily apparent that her husband had no interest in spending any time with her. Except now here he was, acting for all the world as though they dined together on a regular basis.

"That's good to hear. Well?" he said, lifting an eyebrow. "Are you going to eat or not? I hope you're not one of those women who become peckish when a man is present. You're thin enough as it is."

She stared at him in disbelief. "Do you even know you are doing it?"

"Doing what?" he asked brusquely as he cut into his lamb.

"Saying such cruel, insensitive things."

"Me? Cruel and insensitive? Oh all right," he admitted when she merely lifted a brow. "Perhaps, at times, I may come across as a bit…boorish. But I don't do it intentionally. Well, not always."

"A *bit*?" she practically yelped. "Today alone you've insulted me no less than *five* times."

Eric frowned. "The devil I have."

Lifting her right hand, she began to tick off her fingers. "First you complained about my hair, the width of my waist, and the fit of my dress."

"Those were not complaints, they were observations."

"Secondly, you said my gloves were worn–"

"Which is true."

"–and lastly, you said my *entire* wardrobe was out of style." Her hand curled into a fist and struck the table with a light thump. "And that was just from this morning!" A little voice in the back of her mind warned her to stop then and there, but like a boulder that was rolling downhill she only kept picking up momentum. "Do you know you've not said one kind word to me since we've been married? Wait. That is incorrect. You did tell me that Buttercup likes me.

But I believe that is more of a testament to *her* good nature than it is to yours! You are more than boorish. You are rude, and ill-tempered, and – and just plain *mean*!"

"Are you quite finished?" he said in a very soft, very dangerous tone of voice.

Oh dear, Caroline thought as all of the color drained from her face. She'd just shouted. At a *duke*. And not just *any* duke, but her own husband! If he was surly when she was on her best behavior, there was not telling how he would react now.

"Yes," she squeaked as she dropped her hands into her lap and her gaze to her plate. So much for wanting to be a cat! At least a mouse could hide under the table. "I – I believe I am."

"Good." Setting down his utensils with surgical precision, Eric stared at her until she was forced to lift her head. When she did he smiled thinly, but there was no humor in the depths of his frigid blue eyes. "You seem to be under the misguided impression that I owe you something. I do not. I am your husband and you are my wife. It is my duty, as your husband, to provide you with all of the material comforts you could ever possibly wish for. It is your duty, as my wife, to provide me with an heir. That is all I expect of you, and that is all *you* will expect of *me*. Do you understand?"

She bit her lip. "But what – what about love?"

"Love?" he jeered. "Love is a myth. Love is a fallacy. Love is a make believe dream spun by those who would like to believe the world and the people in it are better than they really are. You're a duchess now, Madam. And duchesses do not believe in love."

Something crumpled inside of Caroline. Something small and vulnerable and easily broken. On a breathless sob she threw her napkin to the ground and pushed back from the table.

"Where are you going?" Eric demanded sharply when she stood up. "You have not finished your lamb."

Unable to speak for the tight knot of misery in the middle of her throat, she could only stare at him in wretched silence, her soft gray eyes awash with tears she refused to let fall. Then, for the second time that day, she fled.

WELL THAT HADN'T gone the way he had wanted it to.

Slumping back in his chair, Eric raked a hand through his hair and stared down broodingly into his plate of buttered lamb and roasted asparagus. He'd meant to seduce his wife. Not send her running from the room. But when she'd begun to point out his faults he had automatically gone on the defensive, much like a burly bear poked with a stick. And like a bear, he hadn't been satisfied until he'd drawn blood.

Goddamnit, but he was a bastard. The pain in her eyes when she'd looked at him…it had made his chest ache. Especially since he knew *he* was the one who had put it here.

His appetite gone, he stood up and left the dining room, intending to find Caroline and make amends before she went to bed. But she wasn't in the drawing room. Or the parlor. Or the library. Or her bedchamber, for that matter. Going back downstairs, he entered his private study and rang for Newgate. Within minutes, the butler appeared.

"Yes, Your Grace?" he said, snapping to attention in the middle of the doorway.

"Have you seen my wife?"

Newgate consulted the gold watch he always carried with him in the front pocket of his waistcoat. Eric had given it to him last winter to commemorate his service, and it was one of his most prized possessions. "It is half past six, Your Grace. I believe your wife takes her dinner at this time."

Eric waved his arm. "I was just with her in the dining room. She left and now I can't find her."

The butler concealed his surprise with a well-timed

blink. "You were…dining together?"

"Trying to, at least." Crossing to his liquor cabinet, he poured himself some brandy. "Until she yelled at me," he muttered into his glass before taking a long swallow.

Newgate blinked again. "That doesn't sound like something Her Grace would do. Might I ask what provoked such unusual behavior?"

It was a rather personal question, but then Newgate and Eric had a rather personal relationship. While the late Duke of Readington had been chasing after his wife and drinking himself into a stupor, Newgate had been teaching the future duke everything he needed to know from how to properly tie a cravat to what lure to use when fishing for trout.

Nannies and governesses had come and gone but Newgate had always remained, and over the years he'd become a reliable source of support and wisdom. Much more so than Eric's own father, and certainly more so than his harlot of a mother.

"She said I am cruel and insensitive." Finishing his first glass of brandy, he poured himself another and offered to pour one for Newgate, but the butler shook his head.

"You *are* cruel and insensitive," he said candidly.

Eric scowled. "I am aware, Newgate, thank you.

She claims I never give her compliments. Only insults."

"Do you?"

"I suppose. But it's not my fault she's so bloody sensitive!"

"You seem quite irritated, Your Grace," Newgate observed.

"I *am* irritated." Stalking to the fireplace, he braced an arm against the wooden mantle and glared down into the flames. "She irritates me, Newgate. Like no other woman I've ever known."

"That is readily apparent."

"Well what the devil am I supposed to do about it?"

The butler was quiet for a moment. "I think a better question to ask would be *why* she makes you feel this way. Once you're able to answer that, I believe you'll know what to do."

"Is this another one of your cryptic words of wisdom?"

"I would never presume to give you advice, Your Grace."

"Oh come off it, Newgate. You've been giving me advice for years."

"I haven't the faintest idea what you are talking about," the butler said stiffly.

Leaving his brandy on the mantle, Eric turned around. "Be honest with me, Newgate."

"Always, Your Grace."

"What do you think about her?"

"Your wife?"

"No, the bloody Queen." He rolled his eyes. "Of course I mean my wife."

"I think she is nothing like your mother. And the sooner you realize that, the happier both of you will be." He cleared his throat. "Is there anything else I can help you with, Your Grace?"

Just the mere mention of his mother was enough to make Eric's skin crawl and his shoulders stiffen. Reaching blindly behind him, he picked up his glass of brandy and tipped it all the way back. "If you see the duchess, tell her that I am looking for her."

"I will make sure to do that. Goodnight, Your Grace."

"Goodnight, Newgate." Waiting until the butler had closed the door behind him, Eric sank down into a leather chair and kicked his legs out towards the hearth. Within the brick fireplace the fire crackled and popped, sending little golden sparks flying out through the iron grate. They were too small to cause any harm, most of them burning away into cinders before they ever touched the ground.

Not unlike his marriage.

His mood mellowed by the brandy, Eric was forced to wonder if he wasn't cutting off his nose to spite his face. Newgate was right. Caroline *wasn't* his mother. Lady Eleanor had been selfish and manipulative and shrewd. Caroline was…well, come to think of it he didn't know enough about to her to know *what* she was.

Certainly not selfish, he mused. At least not in a way that was obvious. And if she was trying to manipulate him she wasn't doing a very good job at it. Shrewdness was a bit harder to detect, but he'd yet to see any evidence of that either. Maybe – just maybe – Caroline was precisely what she appeared to be: a shy, awkward wallflower who liked horses and was frightened of her own shadow.

Her little outburst tonight at the table was the first flash of temper he'd seen. He would be lying if he said he hadn't been aroused by it, which was yet another reason why he'd reacted so vehemently. He'd wanted to halt his desire in its tracks before it had time to fester and grow into something he couldn't control. Unfortunately, in his determination to keep his heart closed he may have gone just a bit too far in the opposite direction. Maybe what he needed – what *they* needed – was a course correction.

Not a completely new destination. He'd meant what he said in the dining room. Love was a myth and a fallacy. Love made men weak. Love wasn't meant for dukes…or their duchesses. But there was a difference between love and civility, and surely he could manage to be civil. If only for as long as it took to put a son in her belly. After that there would be no reason to see her at all except for the occasional social outing.

He *did* want to be a good father, but the boy wouldn't need him right away. And he could always have him brought to Readington Crossing for the summers. Caroline could come as well, he supposed. As long as she remained in her wing and he in his.

And she didn't complain about his mistress.

It could work, he decided. It *would* work.

But first he needed to find his wife…and then he needed to bed her.

CHAPTER EIGHT

CAROLINE MANAGED TO avoid her husband for the better part of two days. It made her feel cowardly, but what else could she do? The man was as unpredictable as a winter storm.

And she was tired of being left out in the cold.

It was clear they'd entered their marriage with two very different sets of expectations. She'd wanted to find love and he...well, she really hadn't any idea *what* he had been hoping to find. So she had been avoiding him all together. A short term solution to a long term problem, but it was the only thing she could think to do after everything else she'd tried had failed.

Miserably.

Sinking lower into her bath, she closed her eyes and released a long, heavy sigh. Warm water lapped at her shoulders, covering her pink skin in frothy white bubbles that smelled of lavender and rosemary, an herbal combination that Anne had assured her would ease the tension in her muscles and help her sleep better.

"Come in," she said when she heard a soft knock on the door. "I'm almost finished. Could you lay out my nightdress and wrapper? The ivory with the lace, if you please. Do you think I should leave my hair up or take it down?"

"Take it down," replied a deep, gravelly voice that most certainly did *not* belong to her maid.

"Oh!" Caroline gasped as her eyes flew open. Eric stood at the foot of the tub with his muscular thighs braced apart and his arms folded across his chest. "You – you shouldn't be in here. I – I am not *dressed*," she hissed, beyond mortified to have been caught in such a helpless position.

"Really?" he drawled. "I hadn't noticed." There was a wicked gleam in his eye that she'd never seen before. It sharpened when his gaze raked across the top of the water. "Care for me to join you? The tub looks big enough for two."

Where in heaven's name was Anne? Not that the maid would ever dare come into the bedchamber now that the duke was present. Whether Caroline liked it or not (and she definitely did *not*), she was completely on her own. Just her, her husband, and a handful of rapidly dissipating bubbles.

"No – no," she managed to sputter when he began to untie his cravat. "I – I do not care for that at all. You – you have to leave! This is completely inappropriate!"

One dark eyebrow shot up. "Of course it's appropriate. I'm your husband."

"But I – I don't know you at all!" she said shrilly.

His hands paused. "You're right," he said in a voice that was oddly gentle. "You don't know me and I don't know you. But I thought it was time we remedied that."

"By b-bursting into my bedchamber unannounced?"

His second brow rose to join the first. "I did knock."

"I thought you were the maid!"

"An honest mistake, I suppose. Towel?" he asked, holding one up.

"I am not getting out of the tub while you're standing there *staring* at me," she said incredulously. Just the sheer thought of having Eric see every inch of her naked body was enough to bring a furious blush to her cheeks. When her mother had told her about marital relations she'd said they were done late at night in the dark under the covers. The wife laid very still beneath her husband and closed her eyes and gritted her teeth and it was all over in a matter of minutes. But she'd never mentioned *anything* about bathtubs!

"Well you can't stay in there forever," the duke said reasonably. "You'll catch a cold."

"What do *you* care if I catch a cold?" she muttered, drawing her knees up to her chest and glaring up at him through damp lashes.

He frowned. "I know I haven't been very…welcoming to you, Caroline."

That was the understatement of the century.

"But I can assure you from this point forward I shall endeavor to act more kindly towards you." He hesitated. "There are…things about my past that you don't know. Things that have…well, to put it bluntly, have affected how I view marriage. Because of that I've treated you unfairly, and I would like to strive towards fostering a better relationship between the two of us."

"That's – that's very considerate of you," she said, sheer panic raising her voice an octave when she noted that nearly half of the bubbles were gone. "Let's start tomorrow, shall we?"

"I thought we might start tonight," he said softly, cool blue eyes drinking in the sight of her wet, glossy skin as she did her best to keep herself covered. "Have you ever been kissed, Caroline?"

"K-k-kissed?" she sputtered.

"Yes. Kissed." He took one step towards her, then two, and before she quite knew what was happening he'd sat down on the edge of tub and had his hand in the water, fingers trailing through the bubbles in an absent circle that was creeping dangerously close to her thigh.

"I – I don't know." *Is the water getting hotter*, she thought frantically, *or is it just my imagination?* Suddenly she felt less like a lady enjoying a calm, relaxing bath and more like a boiled lobster. One about to be devoured by a very hungry duke.

"You don't *know*?" he said, amused. "I should hope you would remember. Perhaps it wasn't done properly."

"Perhaps not," she said faintly.

"I've always found the prelude to a kiss to be the most important part. You need to not only make your intentions known, but to set the mood." His eyes, as dark as a stormy sky, slowly traveled over every inch of her wet, quivering body before they settled on her flushed countenance. His mouth curved. "Don't you agree?"

"What – what are you doing?" she demanded when

he rested his forearm on the curved edge of the tub and leaned in close enough for her to smell the muskiness of his cologne, a combination of leather and brandy.

"Setting the mood," he murmured. His hand dipped below the bubbles and she trembled when she felt his fingers brush against her ankle. He began to caress her calf in long, soothing strokes that made her want to stretch like a cat, but she kept her arms wrapped tightly around her knees. "Your skin is soft as rose petals. Tilt your head back, love."

"What? Why?" Her eyes had begun to drift closed, but they snapped open with newfound awareness when he lightly touched her shoulder, the rough pad of his thumb pressing into the delicate hollow of her collarbone.

"Your head. Tilt it back, if you please. I'd like to kiss you now." Equal amounts of humor and raw, naked desire flashed across his face. "If that's all right, of course."

Her belly clenched tight. "I – I suppose," she said nervously. "What should I do?"

"Just tilt your head back," he whispered huskily as his hand slid from her shoulder to the nape of her neck, fingers settling along the rigid lines of her corded muscles, "close your eyes, and enjoy."

As Caroline squeezed her eyes shut, she became increasingly sensitive to the smallest sounds. The water lapping against her thighs. The rustle of Eric's clothing. The soft catch of her own breath. Then his mouth was pressing gently against her mouth and she was being kissed. Not the quick, birdish peck Lord Dunmoore had given her once behind a velvet curtain at his sister's piano recital, but a real, warm, lingering kiss she felt all the way down to the tips of her toes.

It lasted the length of ten thunderous heartbeats before her husband slowly lifted his head and sat back on his haunches. She tried to guess what he was thinking but his expression was guarded, his roguish smile gone.

"Here." Standing abruptly, he picked up the towel he'd left draped over the foot of the tub and held it out to her. "You're going to need this." Then he turned and faced the door, allowing Caroline to emerge from the lukewarm water and quickly dry herself before donning a soft muslin wrapper that clung to the curves of her damp body.

"All right," she said, self-consciously tucking a tendril of hair behind her ear. The rest of it was pinned to the top of her head in a heavy bundle, leaving the nape of her neck exposed. Candlelight brushed up against her side, revealing the dusky rose of one nipple and the long, elegant silhouette of her thigh. "You can turn around now."

Eric turned slowly. Almost reluctantly. His face was cast in shadow, making it impossible for her to decipher what he was thinking. What he was feeling. Then his chin lifted, and his eyes met hers, and the heat in his gaze was so staggering that she felt the blaze of it all the way across the room.

"You're beautiful," he said.

It was not a compliment, but an accusation. One that very nearly prompted an apology to spill from Caroline's lips before she bit her tongue. She had nothing to apologize for. It was not her fault her husband had turned a blind eye to her since their wedding day. Even before that, really. During their courtship she had caught him looking at her from time to time...but he'd never really *looked* at her. At least not like he was doing now. As if she were a tasty rabbit and he was a hungry wolf.

Make that a very large *hungry wolf*, she thought when he took a menacing step forward. His muscular frame seemed to fill the entire room, leaving her with nowhere to run and nowhere to hide. For one wild, heart stopping moment she considered diving under the bed...but she knew it would not stop the duke from claiming what he desired.

He stalked her down with long, prowling strides until nothing stood between them but Caroline's own uncertainty. What had her mother instructed her to do? Suddenly she couldn't remember. Something about gritting her teeth and staring up at the ceiling…

She jolted when Eric touched her hip. Quivered when his hand splayed across the small of her back. Gasped when he yanked her against the hard, hot length of his body.

"I am going to kiss you again." It was not a question this time, but a command, and she scarcely had time to close her eyes and tilt her head back before his mouth was on hers.

He devoured her lips with quick, hungry bites before sliding his tongue between her teeth. She felt her knees wobble from the unexpected sensation, but it was nothing compared to the shock of pure arousal that crashed over her like a wave when his hands slipped beneath her wrapper to touch her breasts.

His thumbs flicked across her nipples, arousing them to pointed, throbbing peaks of desire. Flames licked at her toes and swept up her legs to pool between her thighs. They ignited into a fiery ball of lust when he dipped his head and drew one of her nipples into his mouth, suckling it until her head lolled back and a desperate mewl escaped her lips.

The tiny sound only served to heighten Eric's desire. She caught a glimpse of his eyes, dark and potent and filled with passion, before he swept her up into his arms and carried her effortlessly over to the bed.

With one easy pull her wrapper spilled open, exposing her entire body to his hungry gaze. Overcome with shyness she tried to cover herself, but he gently took her wrist and lifted her arm away from her breasts.

"Don't hide yourself from me." His husky voice rubbed against her skin like rough velvet. Lowering himself to the mattress he kissed her again until the tension in her muscles eased and she was soft and pliant beneath him, her limbs heavy, her breathing deep and even.

Her breaths quickened when he stood up and began to unbutton his shirt. Then she quite simply stopped breathing all together when he lowered his trousers and revealed his throbbing member.

"Oh," she said weakly, shocked – and rather concerned – at the sheer *size* of what awaited her. No wonder her mother had told her to grit her teeth!

"Here, give me your hand," he murmured, and Caroline hesitantly allowed him to wrap her fingers around his warm, silky length. He groaned when her grip reflexively tightened and her gaze darted up to his, a line of surprise furrowing her brow when he seemed to grow even *larger*.

"It's so hard," she said wondrously. "I – I hadn't any idea."

Lady Wentworth had never gone into the exact details of lovemaking which was probably a good thing, for had she told her daughter what to expect Caroline doubted she would have believed her. *That* part of him was supposed to fit *inside* of her?

Impossible.

"I am terribly sorry," she said fretfully, "but I do not see how this is going to work."

The corner of his mouth twitched before he adopted a sober expression. "It will work, love. I assure you."

"But…isn't it going to hurt?"

"No. When done correctly, it should never hurt." Midnight blue eyes glittering with dark, sensual promise, he leaned forward and whispered into her ear, "Unless you want it to."

"I don't," she said hastily.

"Then you've nothing to be afraid of." Devoid of any clothing, he climbed into bed beside her.

Taking a deep breath, she leaned back and centered her head on the middle of a pillow, trying to give herself the best view of the ceiling as possible. Limbs rigid, shoulders stiff, she stared at a wrinkle in the canopy and waited for her husband to do the deed. When he did not climb on top of her and immediately begin thrusting, she glanced at him out of the corner of her eye and frowned.

"Am I doing it wrong?" she asked self-consciously.

Lifting a loose curl from her neck, the duke twisted it absently between his fingers. "Truth be told I haven't the faintest idea *what* you're doing. Bracing yourself for an attack from the French?"

"No." A blush heated her cheeks. "I was…that is to say, I am…I am ready."

"Are you certain?" he queried. When she pressed her lips tightly together and gave a brisk nod, the corner of his mouth lifted in a roguish half smile that had butterflies dancing in her belly. "Well by all means, let's begin."

CHAPTER NINE

NO MAN *LIKED* deflowering an innocent. At least none that Eric had ever met. It was a messy affair, both literally and figuratively. He may not have had any firsthand knowledge, but he'd heard enough horror stories to know that it almost never went well. Gazing down at Caroline, who looked for all the world as if she were a lamb laying on a sacrificial altar, it was not very hard to imagine why.

Mothers, he thought darkly, would do well to keep their traps shut when it came to educating their beloved daughters on the perils of lovemaking. It wasn't *his* fault they'd been forced to sleep with husbands who didn't know a petticoat lane from a tea kettle, and yet he was the one dealing with the consequences.

Sex was not something to be endured. It was something to be enjoyed. That being said, he would be the first to admit he had not been looking forward to bedding his wife.

Getting her pregnant so he could return to London? Yes.

Actually doing the deed? No.

But then he'd kissed her…and everything had changed.

The taste of her lips, the soft mewling cry she'd made when he had cupped her breast, the way she'd melted around him when he had drawn her sweet little nipple into his mouth…had his self-control been any less, he would have fed the growling beast inside of him then and there.

"You needn't be afraid of me, love." He touched her hip and she flinched, her soft gray eyes as wide as he'd ever seen them. "You liked it when we kissed, didn't you?"

The pretty blush in her cheeks intensified. "Yes," she admitted after a pause. "I did. It was…very nice."

"If you relax, this next part will be very nice too. That's it," he murmured when she forced her tiny fists to unclench. "That's a darling." Leaning up on his side, he lowered his mouth to hers and kissed her slowly. Leisurely. As if they'd all the time in the world.

Their legs entwined, her small feet tucking

themselves between his muscular calves. His arousal pulsed against her thigh as he traced the contours of her hipbone before gliding up along her ribcage. When he reached the swell of her bosom he changed direction, fingers dancing down her flat belly and navel to the golden nest of curls that were already damp and awaiting his touch.

She stiffened when he caressed the peak of her womanhood with his fingertip. Softened when he nibbled her earlobe before kissing his way down to her nipples. He took his time, stroking her sensitive bud and suckling her breasts in tandem until she began to move restlessly against him, her body instinctively seeking what it craved but couldn't define. At least not in so many words. But he knew what she wanted, for it was the same thing he desired with every ragged breath he drew into his lungs.

Sheer ecstasy.

Guiding her hand to his cock, he helped her find a steady rhythm. His wife may have been a shy virgin, but she was a quick learner, and with less than half a dozen tentative strokes she had him on the brink of release.

Swallowing a groan, he eased his body on top of hers, one hand tangling in her wild tresses while the other guided his hard, hot length into her. Her eyes flew open and sought his when she felt him nudge at her entrance, but she didn't resist. She couldn't. Like him, she was caught in a thrall neither one of them fully understood.

He slid into her inch by inch, giving her womanhood the time it needed to adjust to his length and girth. And when her delicate brows drew together and her jaw tightened he kissed her grimace away, murmuring sweet, senseless nothings against her lips.

One last slow, steady thrust and he was sheathed completely. Sweat dotted his brow as he held himself perfectly still, waiting for the line across her forehead to ease. When it did – when her nails sank into the coiled muscles in his back and she released a whimpering sob of pleasure – he began to pump in and out, carrying them both towards the edge of a precipice that was higher than any he'd ever known before.

He reached the top first but he waited, waited, waited for her to join him. A finger pressed against the pulsating heart of her desire, a deep, bruising kiss, and she was right there with him, arms flung out, head tilted up towards the blazing sun.

With a desperate cry they both burned together.

THAT, CAROLINE THOUGHT dazedly as she slowly

drifted back down to earth, *was nothing like Mother said it was going to be.*

There had been no staring at the ceiling. No clenching of teeth – at least, not in pain. She hadn't even had to count sheep, or pretend she was doing something far more pleasant, like needlework. Instead she'd reveled in each glorious second, amazed and astonished at the pleasure two human beings were capable of giving to one another.

Wondering if her husband had experienced the same blissful euphoria as she had, she snuck a glance at him from beneath her lashes...and felt a tiny thrill of satisfaction when she saw him sprawled flat on his back with his arms crossed behind his head and a contented smile curling his lips.

Tugging the sheet up to cover her breasts, she turned towards him and gently touched his side, fingers fitting between the grooves in his ribcage. His skin was warm and covered with a silky sheen of perspiration, as was hers.

Lovemaking had been surprisingly rigorous. Not unlike riding a horse, come to think of it, although her husband had done all of the riding. Thank goodness he was such a skilled equestrian!

Biting the inside of her cheek to quell a childish giggle, she let her gaze slowly wander down the rest of his body. In the flickering light of the fire he was all lean muscle and hard lines and golden skin. Having never seen a naked man before, she couldn't help but wonder if this was how they all looked without their clothes on.

Somehow she doubted it.

"Like what you see?" Eric said huskily, and Caroline blushed from the roots of her hair to the tip of her chin when she realized he had been watching her the entire time.

"No. I – I mean yes. I do."

"Good." His dark gaze swept down the length of her willowy frame, lingering on the swell of her breasts beneath the thin sheet. "So do I."

My husband, she decided, *is an absolute cad.*

And she could not have been more delighted.

They may have gotten off to a bit of a rocky start – if by rocks one actually meant enormous boulders – but she knew now that it had all been an act. Eric cared for her. He *must* have, for how else could he have touched her in such an intimate manner? How else could he have whispered so many tender promises in her ear? How else could he have wrung such pleasure from the very depths of her soul?

"Thank you," she said earnestly, her heart swelling with happiness as she sat up on her elbow and beamed down at him. Free of its pins, her hair spilled over his chest in a tangle of curls. Selecting one long tendril, Eric twisted it around his finger.

"For what?" he said absently.

"For loving me." Oblivious to the sudden frost in her husband's gaze, she laughed lightly and leaned down to press a kiss to his cheek. He still smelled of leather and brandy, but there was a new scent on his skin she'd never smelled before.

Her.

"You do not have to say the words if you do not want to." She kissed him once more before sitting up and drawing one long leg to her chest. "At least not right away. I know you prefer to guard your emotions. Eventually it will be nice to hear you say it, of course, but I would never press–"

"I do not love you, Caroline."

Pouring a bucket of ice water on her head would have been kinder.

"What?" she whispered as her smile slowly faded.

"I said I do not love you." Sitting bolt upright, Eric swung his legs over the edge of the mattress and rose to his feet. Snatching his trousers off the floor, he shoved one leg into them and then the other. "I *made* love to you. There is a distinct difference."

"But...but the way you kissed me." Her heart

thumping wildly against her ribcage, she rose to her knees, helpless to do anything but watch as he quickly dressed himself. "All of those things you said to me."

"Are no different than what I've said to a dozen other women. Where the devil is my – here it is." As if he hadn't just plunged a knife into her heart, he pulled his shirt off the back of a chair and yanked it over his head. "This doesn't change anything, Caroline. I am sorry if you thought it would." The pity in his eyes cut a thousand times deeper than his anger ever had. "I meant what I said earlier. I would like to us to maintain a civil relationship. One based on a mutual understanding."

Holding the sheet to her chest as though it was a suit of armor that might somehow protect her from the pain his words were inflicting, she sank back onto her heels. "A mutual understanding of what?" she managed.

"That our marriage will always be one of convenience." His brow furrowed. "I am incapable of love, Caroline. I should think you would have realized that by now."

"Oh," she said softly. "Of – of course."

"It will be better this way, I can assure you."

"Yes," she replied distantly. "Much better."

"You look rather pale," he observed. "Would you

like me to send for your lady's maid?"

"No. I – I am sure I will be fine." *Just as soon as I find a way to stop my heart from aching,* she thought silently.

Eric shrugged. "I shall bid you good evening, then. Sleep well."

"Good evening," she echoed.

But it was a long, long while before she managed to fall asleep.

CHAPTER TEN

"PUT THE EVERGREENS over there," Caroline instructed, pointing to the main staircase, "and bring the holly in here, if you please."

"What are you going to do with it all?" Anne jumped to the side as two footmen, their arms filled with holly, marched into the front parlor. At Caroline's nod they dropped their bushels into two large wicker baskets and went back outside to fetch more.

"Drape it along the mantles and put it in vases." Stepping down off the small ladder she'd been using to hang red bows from the curtain bustles, Caroline put her hands on her hips as she surveyed the room.

After nearly an entire afternoon's worth of decorating, it was coming along quite nicely. A few more finishing touches and it would be ready for Christmas.

One room down. Twenty-two left to go.

Oh well, she thought with a sigh. It wasn't as if she had anything else to occupy her time.

At least not during the day.

As the last of the leaves had fallen and the ground had turned hard and barren, Eric had visited her bedchamber nearly every night. Under the cover of darkness he'd given her more pleasure than she had ever dreamed possible, doing things to her body that made her turn red as a holly berry if she thought of them in the light of day. But when it was over he always left, leaving her to sleep alone in a bed that now felt too large and much too lonely.

She'd tried to console herself with the thought that it was better to have his attention some of the time than not at all, but the truth was she would almost rather he ignore her completely instead of having one husband during the day and a completely different one at night.

When the sun was up he was cold and aloof. If they happened to walk by one another in the hall she felt as though she was passing a stranger. He barely looked at her, let alone touched her. But when the moon rose and he drew her into his arms, it felt as though they'd known each other for their entire lives.

"Are you ready to start on the foyer?" she asked

Anne brightly. "I thought we could weave the evergreen boughs through the bannisters."

But the maid wasn't looking at her, she was looking at the door. As Caroline followed Anne's gaze she felt a familiar ache of longing in her chest when she saw Eric standing in the doorway. He must have just returned from a brisk ride, for his dark hair was windblown and his nose was a tad red.

Over the past few days the temperature had dropped drastically. They'd yet to get any snow aside from a few passing flurries, but with twelve days to go until Christmas she was still hopeful. To her mind there was nothing more beautiful than an estate blanketed in snow. Particularly around the holidays.

This would be the first Christmas she'd ever spent away from home and she didn't know whether to be relieved or sad. She wasn't going to miss the enormous dinner party her mother threw every year, but she'd always loved drinking hot chocolate with her father on Christmas Eve while they tried to guess what was hidden inside their presents.

"Your Grace," Eric said curtly, his keen blue gaze zeroing in on her from across the room. "A word, if you please."

"Of course." Setting down the spool of velvet ribbon she'd been using to decorate the drapes,

Caroline followed her husband out of the parlor and down the hall to the library. A fire crackled in the hearth, giving the room a warm, cheerful glow that was at direct odds with the tightness in her throat.

She hated feeling as though she was always standing on pins and needles whenever she and Eric were in the same room together, but she couldn't help it. Not when she knew he was pretending to be someone he wasn't for reasons she couldn't understand.

She *knew* he wasn't the cold, unfeeling duke he pretended to be. There was warmth in him. Humor as well. Even kindness. But for some reason he always kept the best parts of himself hidden from her, only revealing them when they were completely alone and at their most vulnerable.

It was those parts she had fallen in love with first.

Knowing it was folly, knowing nothing good could come of it but unable to deny the yearning in her heart, she'd committed the worst mistake a woman in the *ton* could possibly commit: falling in love with her own husband.

Every time he touched her, every time he murmured in her ear, every time he wrapped his arms around her and held her to his chest as though he never wanted to let her go, she felt her love for him grow deeper, like roots sinking into the soil.

And every time he left her, every time he saw her enter a room and looked the other way, every time he treated her with distant cordiality instead of desperate passion, the roots were ruthlessly yanked out of the ground.

Then he would come to her in the middle of the night and his hard countenance would soften and he would touch her so sweetly, so gently, that the roots replanted themselves all over again.

It was a cruel cycle. One she was growing wearier of by the day. What she needed – what they *both* needed – was a miracle. And what better time to find one than at Christmas?

"Is something the matter?" she asked when Eric jerked his chin at a chaise lounge in front of the fireplace, indicating she should sit. Perching nervously on the edge, she smoothed out a small wrinkle from her dress as he closed the door.

And locked it.

"Your Grace," she gasped when he pulled off his waistcoat and started to unbutton his shirt. "What – what are you doing?"

"What does it look like I am doing?" he growled as he kicked off his boots.

"But it's the middle of the day!"

"I don't think that's a problem." Before Caroline could muster a reply he had crossed the library and had her flat on her back, one hand pinning her wrists above her head while the other dove up her skirts. "Do you?" he whispered silkily.

"No," she gasped, her spine arching off the chaise lounge as he used two fingers to drive her to a fast, breathtaking orgasm. "I – I don't."

Last night he had lingered over her body for what felt like hours, withholding her pleasure until she was all but begging for him to take her. Now the waves of release came so quickly and with so much intensity that she was left dazed and disoriented when it was finished, her mind numbed to anything but the trembling aftershocks of being thoroughly loved by her husband.

"I am leaving for London first thing tomorrow morning." Standing, Eric pulled on his trousers and reached for his shirt. The muscles in his back bulged and rippled as he tugged the tunic down over his head. "I will be gone for at least a fortnight. Mayhap two." Turning to face her, he raked a hand through his hair, pushing the inky mass off his forehead. "I will send word before I return."

"But Christmas is in twelve days." She'd lost a stocking, Caroline realized as she sat up and straightened her skirts. Drats. That made the third one this week!

"And?"

"And you cannot mean to be gone for *Christmas*." She lifted up one velvet seat cushion, frowned, and then lifted up the other. "Have you seen where my stocking went to? I really can't lose another."

"Here." Bending down, Eric plucked her silk stocking from underneath the chaise lounge and held it out. "Newgate will remain here, so if you require anything you have only to ask him for it."

"You're serious," she whispered. "You're – you're really leaving."

So much for Christmas miracles.

"At first light. What?" he demanded when she gazed silently up at him, gray eyes filled with disappointment. "Why are you looking at me like that?"

"I just thought…this being our first holiday together that…well, that we'd spend it *together*. How foolish of me." Her fingers tightened reflexively around her stocking, nails tearing into the delicate fabric.

A line creased Eric's brow. "If I gave you the impression that we could be spending Christmas together, I apologize."

"No, you didn't. But I assumed…" she trailed off with a dismal shake of her head.

Stupid, she chastised herself. *Stupid, stupid, stupid. Did you honestly believe anything would change, just because it's Christmastime? He did not love you yesterday and he is not going to love you tomorrow, or on Christmas Eve, or on Christmas. He is incapable of love. He said so himself.*

But it did not make the pain any easier to bear.

How much longer could they go on like this? Another month? A year? Indefinitely? Strangers in the daylight, lovers at night. Would it stop when she gave him the heir he so desired? Or would he demand a second? The heir and the spare, so the old saying went. And then what? Would he leave her here to raise their children and grow old by herself while he frolicked in London with his mistresses? Her eyes closed as pain cut through her like a knife, slicing across a heart that was already tender and raw.

"I can't do it any longer." Her eyes opened. "I won't."

"You won't do what?" Eric sat down across from her and began to lace up his boots.

"This. I won't do *this*." She didn't care that her voice was shrill or that it lashed through the library like a whip. The stocking floated to the ground as she leapt to her feet, her diminutive frame vibrating like a plucked bow string with all of the words and emotions she'd been struggling to suppress. "I am not your – your plaything. I am your *wife*!"

"Yes," the duke said with the wariness of someone who realized they'd missed something important, but hadn't the faintest idea what it was. "And I am your husband. I believe that has been thoroughly established. Caroline, why don't you sit back–"

"NO!" she shouted, surprising them both. "I don't want to sit."

"Then stand, but keep your bloody voice down." His eyes narrowed. "And for the love of God do not start crying."

"These are angry tears, you – you – you *dolt*!"

One dark eyebrow shot up. "I'm a dolt now, am I?"

"Yes!" Her heel drove down into the rug for emphasis. "Yes, you are."

"And why is that?" he asked coolly.

"Because you have not figured out that I am falling in love with you! Or maybe you do know, and you simply don't care." She flung her arms in the air. "It does not matter. What matters is that I cannot go on like this any longer! You cannot pick me up when you want me and then put me back on the shelf when you don't. I am not a doll to be played with and then cast aside when the mood strikes."

His eyes flashing a deep, dangerous shade of midnight blue, Eric stood up and towered over her. "I did not realize being my wife was such a hardship for you."

Too incensed to be intimidated, Caroline stiffened her shoulders and jabbed a finger at his chest. "Any woman would find being married to you a hardship! On your very *best* day you are cold, callous, and cruel."

"And yet you claim to be in love me," he scoffed, clearly not believing her.

"I never said it made any sense!"

"If this is about your allowance–"

"Oh!" she cried. "You are the most *infuriating* man I've ever met! Go to London. Stay there for a fortnight. Stay for ten! I don't care. Do you hear me? *I don't care*!" Shoving past him, she ran out of the library and up the stairs to her bedchamber before he could catch a glimpse of her tortured countenance and see that she did care. She cared very much.

But oh, how she wished she didn't.

"STEP OUT OF THE WAY Newgate, I am going for a ride." Stalking across the foyer, Eric threw open the

114

door, admitting a gust of freezing wind so strong that it rattled the windows.

"Another one?" Nonplussed by the tumultuous storm cloud hanging over his employer's head, Newgate pulled a heavy greatcoat out of the closet and held it up. "Might I suggest you wear this, Your Grace."

Glaring out at the frigid landscape, Eric abruptly slammed the door and leaned back against it. Pinching the bridge of his nose, he closed his eyes and muttered a short, savage curse. "She told me that she loved me."

"Your wife?"

"Yes, my wife!" He opened his eyes to glare at the butler. "Do you see a mistress skulking about? My *wife*, Newgate. My *wife* said she was falling in love with me." His brow furrowed. "Then she told me I was cold, callous, and cruel."

"If I may be so bold as to speak openly, Your Grace…"

Eric waved his hand. "Go on then. We both know you're going to say what you want anyways."

The butler returned the greatcoat to the closet before he said, rather bluntly, "You *are* all of those things. And worse."

"Then why the devil would she be in love with

me?"

Newgate shrugged. "Stranger things have been known to happen."

"Do you think it's a ruse to increase her allowance?" He suddenly recalled a conversation he'd overhead between his parents. It was from when they had still been living under the same roof, which meant he'd been a small boy of only five or six. They had been arguing – they were *always* arguing – and his mother had said something that had struck a chord deep inside of him even though he'd been too young to understand what it really meant.

"If you loved me," she'd wept, "you would try to make me happy."

"How am I supposed to do that?" the late Duke of Readington had blustered.

As if someone had turned off a leaky faucet, his mother's tears had immediately stopped. "You could buy me the emerald necklace I saw in the shop window yesterday. Then I would know that you truly loved me."

That was the first time Eric had learned love was not something to be freely given, but something traded. It was a lesson he'd never forgotten…whether he realized it or not.

"Or perhaps she wants a new piece of jewelry," he

said thoughtfully.

"I hesitate to speak on the duchess's behalf, but I do not believe her to be the sort of woman who is interested in material possessions."

Eric's frown turned into a scowl. "Then what the hell does she want?"

"If I may be so bold, I believe what she wants is *you*." A touch of gruffness was detectable in Newgate's voice when he said, "You don't see it, but your wife looks at you the same way my Adelaide used to look at me. True love is a precious gift." Affection for the young man he'd raised as his own son softened the rigid lines around the butler's eyes. "You would do well not to squander it."

CHAPTER ELEVEN

THE STORM ARRIVED with a vengeance. It snowed all through the night, and by the time morning came everything was covered in a heavy blanket of white, including the road to London. Standing with his arms crossed and his legs braced apart, Eric scowled out the drawing room window at the stone drive. Or at least where he imagined the drive to be. Given all the snow, it was impossible to tell precisely where anything was.

He'd already gone out and checked on the horses. They were all tucked safely inside, contentedly eating their hay. But they wouldn't be going anywhere soon.

None of them would.

"Blast and *damn*," he cursed, turning away from the wintry landscape to glare at the hearth. The crackling fire, along with the velvet bows pinned to the curtains and the evergreen boughs draped along the mantle, gave the room a distinctly festive air. His brow creased as he noticed a clump of mistletoe hanging from the door. When the devil had that gotten there?

Stalking over to the doorway, he yanked the mistletoe down and tossed it onto the nearest table. Then he happened to glance out into the foyer and his eyes widened, then narrowed.

Bloody hell.

Mistletoe, holly, and evergreens were *everywhere.*

Dangling down from every doorway, wrapped around the staircase bannister, in vases on the windowsills. There wasn't a drape or a doorway that had escaped decoration.

"You there," he barked at a maid passing by the drawing room. "What's the meaning of this?"

A flicker of fear crossing her face, the maid stopped short. "The meaning of what, Your Grace?"

He gestured around the room with a vague sweep of his arm. "*This*. And that. All of it!"

"Oh." The maid's nervous frown gave way to a beaming smile. "Isn't it lovely, Your Grace? Why, I cannot recall a time the manor has ever looked so festive! Have you seen the gingerbread house in the solarium yet?"

Eric blinked. "The ginger what?"

"It's absolutely marvelous," the maid gushed. "Why, Her Grace even made little gingerbread men!"

His jaw tightened. For most people, Christmas was

a time of joy and celebration. But the winter holiday had never brought him much joy, and listening to his parents scream at one another had hardly been cause for celebration.

On the rare occasion his mother hadn't been in the arms of another man and his father had been sober enough to recall what day it was, they'd managed to have breakfast together as a family, but that was always where the revelry ended. There had never been any opening of presents in front of the fireplace, or kissing under the mistletoe, or burning the yuletide log. And there'd certainly never been any gingerbread men.

"Where is she?" he growled.

"I – I believe Her Grace is still in her bedchamber," the maid squeaked. "Is there anything I can–"

But he was already gone.

"ANNE, COULD YOU leave us please?" Caroline said calmly when her husband stormed into her bedroom, his face as dark as a storm cloud and his steely eyes flashing with temper.

Dropping the comb she'd been using to style Caroline's hair into a neat chignon, the maid was only too happy to scurry from the room. She closed the door neatly behind her, and in the brittle silence that followed her departure the quiet *click* of the tumbler falling into place sounded like a gunshot.

Drawing her robe more closely around her shoulders, Caroline met Eric's hard gaze in the silvery reflection of her dressing mirror. *Like Perseus and Medusa,* she thought, the corners of her mouth twitching. An apt comparison, given how Gorgonesque her husband had been acting as of late. If only defeating him could be so easy. Cutting off a monster's head was a straightforward endeavor. Melting a duke's heart was much more difficult.

Mayhap even impossible.

Picking up the comb Anne had dropped, she began to work it through her long hair, careful not to let the ivory spines catch on any tangles. "I see you have not yet left for London."

He jerked an irritable shoulder at the window. "We are completely snowed in. I wouldn't be surprised if the roads were not cleared until well after Christmas." He paused. "I see you have been decorating."

Surprised that he had noticed, she inclined her head ever-so-slightly. "There are still the second and third floors to be done, but the first is nearly finished. I'd planned on completing the library this afternoon."

"Why?"

"Why what?"

"Why are you decorating?" he asked between gritted teeth. "No one asked you to."

"Because it is Christmas," she said, as if it were the most obvious answer in the world. "I did not realize I needed your permission."

"You don't. It's just…never mind," he muttered, glancing away from the mirror as a muscle ticked in his jaw.

Caroline frowned. "Do you not like Christmas?"

"No. Not particularly."

"But it is the happiest time of the year," she said, aghast at the idea of someone disliking *Christmas*. Who didn't love a house that smelled of fresh evergreens and carolers singing by candlelight and finding the perfect yuletide log to burn in the hearth?

"For you, perhaps. But not for me."

"How can you hate Christmas?" she asked, genuinely puzzled. "It's a time of joy and giving. Of celebration and festivity. Of hope and–"

"I get the bloody idea," he said curtly. "Not everyone was raised in the same fairytale family as yours. For some of us Christmas is simply another day."

She barely managed not to snort. "I would hardly call my family a fairytale. You've met my mother."

"And you should consider yourself lucky that you've never met mine."

Something in the way he spoke caught her attention. Her winged brows drew together over the bridge of her nose. "I...I am afraid I do not understand. I thought your mother was…"

"Deceased?" he drawled when she hesitated. "Hopped the twig? Popped her clogs? Gone to a sticky end?"

Caroline gasped. "I really don't think you should speak of the dead in such a manner. Especially your own mother."

"The old witch isn't dead." He rubbed his chin. "Or at least I don't think she is."

"You mean you do not *know*?"

"How would I? We haven't spoken in nearly ten years after she made it clear that her various lovers were more important than her own sons." Although he managed to keep his voice steady, he couldn't quite disguise the flash of pain in his eyes. "Your Christmases may have been spent roasting chestnuts by the fire, but I can assure you I do not have such happy memories."

It was the first time Eric had ever revealed anything of a personal nature, and her heart ached for the boy whose mother had been so callously selfish that she had preferred the company of another man to her own children.

No wonder Eric held love in such bitter disregard! Her own mother was hardly perfect, but at least Caroline knew that she was loved. What would it have been like to grow up without that assurance? Terribly lonely, she imagined. No wonder her husband thought himself incapable of love. How could he know what it felt like to love someone if he'd never been loved himself?

As a new sense of understanding for the complicated man she'd married softened the hard edges of her anger, she set her comb aside and gathered her long mane at the nape of her neck. "Would you mind helping me?" she asked softly. "Anne makes it all look so easy, but I fear fashioning a chignon is much more difficult than it appears." Her lips curved in a self-deprecating grin. "Or perhaps I would simply make a poor lady's maid."

Eric crossed the room to stand behind her and she felt her spine tingle with awareness when he gently rested his hands on her shoulders, warm fingers sliding beneath the lace edge of her dressing robe.

"What do you need me to do?" Their eyes met in the mirror, pale gray sinking into deep, dark blue. She saw the arousal in his gaze. Felt it in the heat pulsing from his body. Heard it in the husky velvetiness of his voice. If only she could magically turn his lust into love! There was plenty of it to spare. But of course it wasn't that simple. Nothing worth having ever was.

"Just hold – hold this pin," she said, her breath catching when his thumbs slowly traced along the edges of her collarbones.

"There's only one problem," he murmured, his breath warming her cheek as he leaned in close. He smelled of brandy and the faintest hint of peppermint. Heat pooled between her thighs and she squirmed on the velvet stool as a wave of desire swept up through her body, threatening to drown out all common sense.

"What – what is that?" she asked weakly.

"I like your hair down." He slowly drew her hands away from her hair and it tumbled down her back in a curtain of burnished gold. Sweeping it to the side, he started to kiss his way down her neck, but when his hand slipped between the folds of her dressing robe and cupped her breast she stiffened.

"W-wait," she gasped as logic pushed against longing. "This will not solve anything."

"I can think of at least one thing it will solve," he said meaningfully, capturing her wrist and placing her hand on his hard phallus.

She began to touch him through his breeches, her

head falling back on a moan of pleasure as he captured her mouth and boldly slid his tongue between her lips in a series of long, drugging kisses that left her dazed and disoriented.

His hand slid between her thighs and they fell open. She was already damp with need. He growled his approval as he parted her curls and began to stroke the sensitive bud nestled above the heart of her femininity. Six long, sensuous slides of his finger against her quivering flesh and she was completely lost.

Logic? What was logic when she had passion? This was what she craved, after all. To feel desired above anything or anyone else. To feel *needed*. Need was a poor substitute for love, but in the moment it was all she had…and she clung to it with the desperation of a drowning sailor trying to keep his head above water.

Her palms bit into the marble edge of the dressing table when he dragged her to her feet. Drunk on desire, she vaguely heard the crash of the stool as he kicked it aside. She hissed out a breath when he hiked up her robe and the cool air brushed against the back of her legs, but then he plunged himself into her warm, wet sheath and there was only heat.

CHAPTER TWELVE

"I – I DID NOT REALIZE you could make love like that." Feeling suddenly, inexplicably shy, Caroline busied herself with straightening everything that had been knocked askew on the dressing table during their…exertions.

Eric grinned at her in the mirror as he tugged on his breeches. "There are all kinds of ways to make love. We've hardly scratched the surface."

Her interest piqued, she stole a quick glance at him over her shoulder. "Do you know all of them? The ways, that is."

"Hardly." Wrapping an arm around her waist, he yanked her against his chest. "But luckily for you, I've decided to devote myself to learning each and every one," he whispered throatily into her ear.

A blush stole across Caroline's cheeks. "That's – that's very naughty of you."

He bit her neck. "I know."

She watched snow fall from the pale, moody gray sky as she remained wrapped in the duke's arms, content to listen to the shallow rasp of his breaths and the steady thump of his heartbeat. He was warm and comforting and on a soft sigh she let her head fall back against his chest as her eyes drifted closed and a small smile curved her mouth.

This was all she wanted. To feel loved. To feel special. To feel like a real *wife*, not a mistress to be picked up and discarded when the mood struck.

"This is nice," she murmured, but no sooner had the words left her lips than Eric let her go and stepped back. Bereft of his body heat, she shivered as she turned, fingers sinking into her ribcage as she hugged her arms around herself. Then she saw his expression. His cool, distant expression. And she shivered for another reason all together.

"You may decorate the first floor as you see fit," he began, speaking in the detached tone of a lord addressing a servant instead of a woman he'd just been inside of. "But leave the second and third floors alone. I won't have my bedchamber filled with holly and mistletoe and God only knows what else."

This time her heart didn't ache.

It shattered.

"It will never be any different, will it?" she whispered as tears born of misery and despair burned the corners of her eyes. "You and I. Our marriage. It will never change."

"If the bloody evergreens mean that much to you–"

"It isn't about the evergreens!" she burst out. "I mean I suppose it is, a little bit. But it really isn't."

His eyes narrowed. "You're not making a damn bit of sense."

"And neither are you! How can you hold me so tenderly one moment and speak to me so coldly the next? Am I nothing more than a – a warm body to you?"

"Do not be ridiculous," he scoffed. "You're my wife."

"Your wife. Your *wife*." Hysteria bubbled up inside of her, pitching her voice up an octave and curling her hands into fists of bewildered outrage. "I am no more your wife than you are my husband. You said it yourself! This marriage is nothing but one of convenience."

"And?" he said expectantly.

"Oh!" Reaching blindly behind her, she picked up the first thing within reach and launched it at her husband's head. The perfume bottle missed by several feet and crashed against the wall, filling the bedchamber with the scent of honeysuckle and night jasmine. "If you were too thick-skulled to understand the first time, I am not going to waste my breath explaining it once more!"

"Now see here," he growled, but she jumped back when he reached for her.

"No." Hair whipped across her cheek as she shook her head from side to side. "You're not going to lull me into complacency with your – your charm and your kisses. Not again!"

"Lull you into…what the devil are you talking about?"

"I am sorry your mother did not love you the way you needed her to."

Eric's eyes flashed a deep, ominous blue black. "This has nothing to do with my mother."

"*Of course it does!*" she shrieked, and for the first time a genuine flicker of alarm crossed the duke's countenance.

"Caroline–" he began, but she was not having any of it. Having gone this far, she wasn't going to stop until she finally said what was in her heart. Her poor, battered, broken heart.

"Don't 'Caroline' me. You may be blind to the fact that whatever poor relationship your parents had has given you a misguided notion of what love should be, but I'm not." She drew a deep breath.

"I *know* you are capable of more than what you're giving. I've felt it when you touch me. I've seen it in your eyes when you look at me. It would be easier if you really *couldn't* love me. But I know you can. I know it." Tears spilled from her lashes and streamed down her face. "You just don't want to."

"Caroline–" he tried again, but she no longer wanted to hear what he had to say.

"Please leave," she said hoarsely.

"I really think we should–"

"*Leave.*"

"Fine." He squared his shoulders. "You know, I am beginning to think this is really a marriage of *in*convenience. I never should have picked you." And with that last cold, cutting remark, he turned on his heel and strode from the room.

CAROLINE ALLOWED HERSELF precisely one hour of self-pity. Then she picked herself up off the bed, dusted herself off, and walked out of her bedchamber as if nothing were amiss. If her husband truly did not love her – which he'd just proven yet again – then she wasn't going to waste another second's worth of time and energy trying to convince him otherwise. And she most certainly was not going to allow him to ruin

Christmas.

Thankfully the manor was very large, and over the next few days she only saw Eric twice. Once while she was having breakfast in the solarium and she glimpsed him walking out to the barn, and another time when she ducked into the library late at night to pick out a book to help her sleep.

He'd been reading in front of the fire and they'd both caught the other off guard. For the span of a heartbeat their gazes had met before she'd snatched a book blindly off the shelf and fled with what little dignity she had left.

During the day she kept herself busy by decorating every nook and crevice she could wedge a piece of holly into, and by the time Christmas Eve dawned the house was nearly complete.

Candles burned in every window, clumps of mistletoe hung from every doorway. There was garland twisted through all of the bannisters and red bows pinned to the drapes. A large wreath hung on the front door and a matching one had been nailed to the mantle in the drawing room.

There was only one thing missing.

"You there," she called out brightly to a footman. "Could you have Buttercup saddled for me, please?"

"You're going for a ride *now*?" Emerging from the

parlor balancing a silver tea tray, Anne glanced out the window. "But it will be dark in a few hours. And it's cold." Her nose wrinkled. "And *snowing*."

Caroline wrapped a long wool scarf around her neck and drew up the hood of her fur-lined cloak. "I will not be gone long and I won't be going very far. Just to the tree line and back."

"If it's fresh air you're after the footmen have shoveled a path around the garden. Why not a short walk instead?" her maid suggested. "I don't know if His Grace would want you riding out alone."

Caroline's mouth thinned. "His Grace doesn't give a donkey's behind *what* I do."

"That's not true," Anne protested.

She lifted a brow. "Isn't it? I won't be gone long. I promise."

"But where are you going?" Anne called out as Caroline opened the front door and stepped out into the lightly falling snow.

"The Yule log!" she called back over her shoulder. "I am going to get the Yule log."

CHAPTER THIRTEEN

"WITH ALL DUE respect, you cannot hide in here forever, Your Grace."

Looking up from the ledgers he'd been tallying, Eric scowled at his butler. "I am not hiding," he growled as he pushed his chair back and stood up. "I am working."

"And I suppose it is just a coincidence that you have been 'working' ever since you and Her Grace had a falling out?" Newgate asked.

"How the bloody hell do you know about that?"

"Aside from the fact that you have both been taking great pains to avoid one another for the better part of a week, Her Grace's bedchamber still smells like perfume. Adelaide threw a candlestick at my head once," he said, smiling vaguely at the memory.

Walking around to the front of his desk, Eric crossed his arms and leaned back against it. "What did you do?"

"Before or after I regained consciousness?" the butler said dryly.

It wasn't often that Newgate spoke of his wife, who had died nearly eight years ago of consumption. She had been a sweet woman, constantly sneaking Eric biscuits when she thought her husband wasn't looking. Which of course he always had been. There wasn't very much that escaped the butler's notice, then or now.

Including the dismal state of my marriage, Eric thought silently. Picking up a feather tipped quill, he twirled it absently between his fingers.

"You and Adelaide seemed happy, Newgate."

The aging butler inclined his head. "We were, Your Grace. Very much so. I miss her every day."

He touched the quill to his chin. "My parents were never happy."

"No," Newgate agreed. "I fear they were not."

Eric was silent for a long moment. After his fight with Caroline he'd been filled with righteous anger. He'd made it clear what their marriage was and what is wasn't, had he not? Why couldn't she be content with what he *could* give her, instead of dwelling on what he couldn't? But then his anger had faded, and he'd felt…lost. Empty. Alone. And the only thing he'd wanted to fill the void in his heart was Caroline.

Whether by accident or design, his little wife had gotten under his skin in a way no other woman ever had. He didn't just want her body. He wanted her smile. He wanted her laughter. He wanted her blushes. He wanted the shy glances she snuck in his direction when she thought he wasn't looking. Until she had taken them away he hadn't realized how much they'd come to mean to him. How much *she* had come to mean to him.

If that wasn't love, then devil take it he didn't know what was.

"I saw what my mother did to my father," he said slowly. "The pain she put him through. The ultimatums she gave him. I thought that's what love was. What it looked like. What it meant. But now I don't think it is. Love isn't something to be bartered or traded. It isn't a weapon or a means to get something you want. It can't be found in an emerald necklace or a pint of ale." He met Newgate's steady gaze. "I was so bloody determined not to turn into my father that I became my mother. But I don't want to be either one of them. Not anymore. Do you think Caroline and I could be happy together? That we could love one another, as you and your Adelaide did?"

"Respectfully, Your Grace, that is a question only

you can answer."

Eric's chest tightened as he recalled the misery in Caroline's beautiful gray eyes when she'd poured out her heart to him.

'I know you are capable of more than what you're giving. I've felt it when you touch me. I've seen it in your eyes when you look at me. It would be easier if you really couldn't love me. But I know you can. I know it. You just don't want to.'

"I think I already have, Newgate." He dropped the quill, picked up his coat, and, much to Newgate's astonishment, gave the butler a two-armed embrace that left the older man gasping for breath. "I think I already have."

WHERE THE DEVIL did I leave it? Caroline asked herself, borrowing one of her husband's favorite curses as she steered Buttercup between two towering pines. Her head bent and her ears flattened against the brisk wind, the draft mare trudged gamely through the snow as they wound their way deeper and deeper into the woods.

They'd been walking for what felt like hours, searching in vain for the short, stout log that Caroline had left propped against an old stump the last time she'd ventured this far into the forest. Of course there hadn't been any snow then…and it hadn't been nearly as cold, or as dark. With a shiver she pulled gently on the reins and Buttercup came to a halt, twin plumes of smoke rising up from her nostrils as she lifted her neck.

"I am terribly sorry," Caroline said apologetically, reaching down to brush flakes of snow off the mare's scruffy mane. "I did not think it would take this long. If I could just find where I left it…" She brought a hand to her brow and scanned their surroundings, but with everything covered in a blanket of white it was impossible to decipher one log from the next.

The one she was looking for was much smaller than a traditional Yule log, but that was why she'd picked it. So she could easily drag it back herself. In hindsight she wished she'd sent a group of footman to carry out the task for her. But there was nothing she could do about it now…except to turn back around.

Collecting up the reins, she nudged her frozen feet into Buttercup's sides and the mare started walking again. But they'd gone no more than ten feet before Caroline pulled her up once more, a flicker of unease coiling in her belly when she realized she hadn't the faintest idea what direction they were traveling in. She'd thought the manor was behind them. Or was it in front of them? With the snow on the ground and more falling from the sky every minute, she could no longer be certain.

"Oh dear," she fretted. "I never should have come out here."

Maybe if she allowed Buttercup her head the mare would know how to get them back to the barn. But when she loosened the reins and gave a light kick the draft merely turned and looked up at her with large, unblinking brown eyes as if to say, *'You got us into this mess and it's your job to get us out'*.

"You're right. Of course you're right. The manor is…that way!" she decided, pointing at a cluster of pine trees that looked vaguely familiar. Drawing her cloak more snugly around her shoulders, she urged Buttercup onwards through the snow with an encouraging cluck of her tongue.

After two wrong turns and one frightening slide down an embankment, they finally stumbled out of the forest and Caroline breathed an enormous sigh of relief when she saw lights twinkling in the distance.

"See?" she said, leaning down to give Buttercup a teeth chattering hug. "I knew we could do it!"

But no sooner had they set off across the field than an icy chill of warning swept down her spine.

And then the wolves began to howl.

CHAPTER FOURTEEN

"YOU THERE. Have you seen my wife?"

Anne stopped dusting the mantle. She turned to find the duke standing just inside the drawing room, hands tucked into the pockets of his trousers and a deep line creasing his brow.

"She hasn't returned yet?" Her gaze darted to the window, but it was so dark the only thing she could see was her own reflection. "Oh no. I didn't realize she had been gone this long."

"Gone?" the duke snapped, dark brows pinching above the bridge of his nose. "What the devil do you mean she's gone? Gone where?"

"The woods." As worry for the duchess drained the color from her cheeks, the feather duster went clattering to the floor. "She's gone into the woods to look for a Yule log. But she left hours ago. I did not realize – oh!" she gasped when the duke crossed the room and grabbed her by the shoulders.

"What direction?" he demanded, his expression fiercer than she'd ever seen it. "What direction did she go? Answer me, damn you!"

"The field behind the stables. I – I think she went to the field!"

With a vicious curse the duke let her go, and Anne ran after him into the foyer.

"Do you think she's in d-danger?" she asked, her voice trembling with fear at the thought of something perilous having happened to her dear friend.

"I don't know." Forgoing a jacket or even a cloak, he pulled on his riding boots and then disappeared into his study. Less than a minute later he emerged, and her eyes widened when she saw what he was carrying.

"Is that a–"

"Pistol. Stay right here in case she returns. Do not move from that spot. Do you understand?"

Anne nodded jerkily. "Yes," she whispered. "I understand."

A gust of freezing wind and snow swept into the foyer when he opened the front door. "If I am not back in half an hour sent out the footmen."

"Which one?"

"All of them," he said grimly.

BUTTERCUP WHIRLED AND SNORTED as the howls grew ever closer. Clinging to her mount's neck with all the strength her frozen fingers could muster, Caroline fought desperately to keep a cool and level head.

"Easy girl. It – it will be all right." But even to her own ears her words sounded hollow.

Oh, *why* hadn't she listened to Anne? A walk around the gardens would have been a thousand times better than cowering in the darkness waiting to be devoured by wolves! But she had been so determined to have the perfect Christmas that she'd ignored the dangers of going into the woods by herself, and now she was paying the ultimate price for her stupidity.

Had anyone even noticed she was gone? Anne, perhaps, but certainly not her husband.

Eric is probably glad *I am going to be eaten*, she thought bitterly.

There was a loud rustle behind them and Buttercup spooked, spinning to the left as Caroline, not expecting the sudden movement, flew off to the right.

She landed on her backside, her fall cushioned by the snow. Clumsily trying to find her footing, she managed to stand just in time to watch the terrified draft mare gallop away across the field.

"Blast and *damn*," she cried, pounding her fist into the palm of her hand. Another eerie howl had every hair on the back of her neck rising straight up, and with a frightened gasp she tried to run for the woods, but the snow was too deep.

Helpless to do anything but try to defend herself, she picked up a long stick and swung it like a sword as she spun in a circle, desperately searching the inky darkness for any hint of the vicious beasts that prowled and stalked.

Her heart was pounding so loudly she feared it was going to burst from her chest and no matter how hard she sucked cold, icy air into her lungs she couldn't seem to catch her breath. A flicker of movement caught the corner of her eye and a shrill scream burst from the depths of her throat, but it was nothing more than a skeletal branch blowing in the breeze.

Or so she hoped.

"Please don't eat me," she pleaded desperately. "I – I don't think I would taste very good."

But if the wolves heard her – or cared – they gave no sign.

Just as she was about to give up all hope, a single gunshot rang through the night followed by the thunderous pounding of hooves.

"Buttercup?" she called out, squinting into the shadows.

But it wasn't the draft mare who came cantering to her rescue.

It was her husband.

"Grab my hand," he ordered tersely, and with little other choice but to obey his command Caroline latched onto his arm as he rode past. She was swept effortlessly into the saddle and then they were galloping back to the manor, leaving the wolves far behind as Eric's stallion cut easily through the deep snow, his long legs doing what Buttercup's shorter limbs could not.

"B-Buttercup?" Caroline asked, forcing the horse's name out between chattering teeth. "Is –is she all right?"

"She's back at the stables." His jaw clenched, Eric did not look at her or speak again until they'd reached the front door. He swung his powerful thigh over the side of the saddle and dismounted first, but before Caroline could do the same he had her in his arms and was carrying her up the steps and into the foyer. Anne was there to greet them and her face lit up with relief when she saw Caroline was alive and well.

"You're back! Oh, thank goodness. I was so–"

"*Go. Away*," Eric snarled.

"Yes Your Grace," the maid squeaked before she turned on her heel and scurried off, a small animal seeking shelter from the storm that was about to be unleashed.

Caroline squirmed in her husband's arms. "You can put me down now," she said, her voice muffled against his hard chest. "I am perfectly capable of walking."

"No," he bit out as her carried her through the foyer and down the hall to the library. "In fact, I may never put you down again!" To prove his point he sat down in one of the large leather chairs facing the fireplace, but he still did not loosen his grip.

Muttering something undecipherable under his breath, he sat her on his lap while he untied her cloak and pulled off her scarf and mittens. For her part Caroline held perfectly still, not wanting to give him a reason to become even angrier with her than he already was.

He did not speak to her again until he'd stripped away all of her wet outer garments and wrapped a blanket around her shivering body. Sitting her on the floor directly in front of the fire, he sat behind her, his thighs pressing against her hips as he drew her back against his chest in an embrace that, if she didn't know any better, she would have thought of as protective.

"You could have been killed," he said flatly.

She shivered. "I know."

"A few more minutes and those wolves would have ripped you to pieces."

"I know."

"You risked not only your life, but your horse's as well."

"I *know*." She twisted in his arms and glared up at him through her lashes. "It was stupid of me to ride off by myself. Stupid and foolish and I will never do it again. Although I don't see why you would care if I was killed or not," she muttered under her breath.

"What did you say?" he asked sharply.

She sat up a little straighter. "I *said* I don't see why you would care if I was killed or not!"

Firelight danced across the muscle ticking in his jaw. "Of course I would bloody well care!"

"That's right, you still need an heir, don't you? Next time I will make certain not to risk my life until *after* I've given you a son." Ignoring her aching muscles, she jumped to her feet, and Eric did the same.

Had someone told Caroline when she first married the duke that she would one day square off with him as if she were a boxer stepping into the ring, she would have laughed at the absurdity of it. *Her*, standing up to *him*? Yet here she was, chin angled, hands curled into fists, gray eyes sharp with temper.

"Admit it," she hissed. "I am nothing more than a glorified broodmare. *That's* the only reason you rescued me. Out of some sense of – of obligation! You would have done better to have left me in the field."

"Left you to be eaten by wolves?" he said incredulously.

"At least they wouldn't have toyed with me first!"

"No, they would have devoured you in two bites. One if they were particularly hungry." He raked a hand through his hair, pulling the ends taut. Then the hard lines of his countenance abruptly softened. "Caroline–"

"Don't," she warned, pointing her finger at him. "This is not going to end with my heels up by my head!"

Roguish interest stirred in his gaze. "We haven't tried that position before."

"And we are not going to!" She stomped her foot. "Stop *looking* at me like that!"

"Like what?" he challenged huskily as he stepped forward, crowding her back against a side table. A vase filled with red holly berries wobbled and nearly fell over when Caroline bumped the table with her hip. She crossed her arms over her chest; a pitiful defense against his scorching stare but it was the only one she had.

"I know exactly what you are doing and I am not going to fall for it. Not this time."

"That's too bad," he said quietly. "Because I am falling for you."

"I meant what I said in my bedchamber and I – what?" she said blankly when his words finally registered through the angry fog she'd wrapped herself in. "You're what?"

His blue eyes never leaving hers, he reached out and took her small hands into his larger ones. "I am falling for you," he repeated, gently squeezing her fingers. "I am sorry it has taken me this long to realize it. I know I have not been a good husband, but if you give me the chance I can do better. I *will* do better."

Caroline felt a flicker of hope blossoming amidst the broken shards of her heart...but then she remembered everything he had done, and everything he had said, and she grabbed the hope and yanked it out before it could take root.

"I don't believe you." Snatching her hands away, she side-stepped around the table and began to edge towards the door. "You're just saying those things so I will be intimate with you again."

"No I'm not. Well, yes I am," he admitted, cupping the back of his neck, "but if you would just hear me out–"

"I am not interested in anything you have to say."

He scowled at her. "I am trying to bare my heart to you. The least you could is listen."

"The least *I* could do? What makes you think I owe you anything?" she said incredulously.

"You're right. You do not owe me–"

"You have made my life miserable since the moment you placed this ring upon my finger!" Firelight reflected off the plain gold band when she lifted her hand. "Did you honestly think a few words are enough to fix everything? I meant what I said before. You are a cold, callous, cruel man. And it was my fault for believing you could ever be anything else."

Before she could change her mind, she yanked the ring off and threw it at the fire with all of her might. Cursing, Eric leapt forward and tried to catch it before it fell into the flames, but she didn't bother to wait and see if he had. For all she was concerned, it could burn right along with the rest of their marriage.

She was done.

CHAPTER FIFTEEN

CHRISTMAS MORNING DAWNED cold and bright. Having spent a restless night tossing and turning, Caroline considered pulling the blankets up over her head and sleeping the day away. But it was Christmas, and even if the last thing in the world she felt like doing was celebrating, she couldn't ignore the holiday. Not when it was the only bright spot in an otherwise dismal month.

"Anne," she called out, muffling a yawn as she sat up. "I'd like to get ready now." Her pale eyebrows knitted together when there was no response. "Anne?" she said uncertainly. "Are you there?"

Perhaps the maid was down the hall. But when she hurriedly tiptoed across the freezing floorboards and opened her door, she didn't see hide nor hair of Anne.

In fact, she didn't see anyone.

"That's peculiar," she muttered, casting a quick glance left and then right. The main hallway, usually a bustle of activity in the morning, was completely empty. Ducking back into her bedchamber, she quickly pulled on a pair of thick wool socks and knotted her dressing robe closed at the waist. Leaving her hair trailing down her back in a tangle of blonde curls, she went downstairs to discover the first floor was just as devoid of servants as the second had been.

"Hello?" Confused, she turned in a slow circle. Where was everyone? "Is anyone here? Anne? Mr. Newgate? Cook?"

"I gave them all the day off."

Caroline nearly jumped out of her socks when Eric suddenly appeared behind her. "Oh," she gasped, slapping a hand over her racing heart as she whirled to face him. "You scared me!"

"Sorry," he said, although he didn't look very apologetic. "That was not my intention."

Casually dressed in a white linen shirt and a pair of gray trousers with his hair damp and curling from a recent bath, he looked as handsome as she'd ever seen him. Not that she was looking. Because she wasn't. Not at all.

Well, maybe a little bit.

"What – what is going on?" she demanded, forcibly tearing her gaze away from the V of golden skin at the base of his neck. "Where is everyone?"

"Follow me," he said mysteriously, before he turned and started walking briskly in the direction of the library.

"Wait! I do not understand – stubborn man," she broke off under her breath when it became clear he had no intention of stopping. Picking up the hem of her nightgown she hurried after him, feet slipping and sliding on the polished floor.

Slightly out of breath, she managed to catch up to him just as he reached the library. "What are we doing here?" she asked. "And why is the door closed? It is never closed. Are Anne and Mr. Newgate in there?"

The corners of his mouth twitched. "To answer your second question no, your maid and my butler are not in there. As for your first, I thought this would be a fitting place to have it. After all, aside from your bedchamber this is where we've spent most of our time together. Granted the majority of it has been spent arguing, but I hope after today that will begin to change."

She shook her head. "A fitting place to have *what*?"

"Christmas, of course." He pushed open the door and then stepped to the side, allowing her an unfettered view of the library. What she saw took her breath away. There, taking up most of the fireplace, was the largest Yuletide log she had ever seen. And tied around the middle was a bright red bow.

"I don't...I don't understand." Eyebrows pulling together in bewilderment, she looked back at Eric over her shoulder. "Where – where did this come from?"

"The forest."

"I *know* that. I meant what is it *doing* here?"

He walked past her into the library and then turned so they were standing face to face. "I cut it down and brought it here for you," he said simply as he reached out and gently tucked a loose curl behind her ear. For a moment the back of his hand lingered on the soft curve of her cheek and it took all the self-restraint she possessed not to close her eyes and lean into his touch.

It's an act, she told herself fiercely. *It's all an act. Do not let him play you for a fool. Not again.*

"If you did this as some sort of trick to try and seduce me–"

"I did this," he interrupted, "because you were right."

She blinked. "I – I was?"

"Yes."

"About what?"

His grin was charmingly sheepish. "Everything, mostly. But especially what you said last night about a few words not changing anything. I meant what I said, Caroline. I *am* falling in love with you. Or maybe I already have." He shrugged. "I've never been in love before, so I'm not really sure."

"Your Grace–"

"Eric," he said. "If we are going to become engaged, I think you should call me Eric."

"Engaged?" she echoed, truly at a loss. "But we're already married!"

"No we're not. You married the Duke of Readington."

"You *are* the Duke of Readington." Her eyes narrowed with suspicion as she took a step back. "Are you foxed? Is that why you're acting so oddly?"

"I am not foxed and I am not the Duke of Readington." His gaze hardened. "The Duke of Readington is a cold-hearted bastard who wouldn't know what love was if it ran him over in the street. He doesn't deserve his wife, and she bloody well doesn't deserve him. His wife is kind, and intelligent, and beautiful, while he is–"

"A dolt?" she suggested.

"Yes," he agreed without hesitation. "He's a right proper dolt."

"And who is Eric?" she asked softly as a tendril of warmth began to unfurl inside of her chest, spreading up through her lungs and surrounding the ice that had hardened around her heart.

"Eric is a man who wants a second chance. He knows he's not entitled to it, but he prays to God you'll give it to him nevertheless. I love you, Caroline," he said huskily. "I am sorry it took me this long to realize it. And I am sorry, so bloody sorry, that I've treated you as though you meant nothing to me."

"Eric–"

"You were never nothing, Caroline." His blue eyes steady on hers, he closed the distance between them. "You were always everything. And that terrified me because I didn't want to end up like my father, in love with a woman incapable of loving him back. But what I understand now, that I didn't before, is whatever my parents had, it was never love." He took her hands. Squeezed them tight. "*This* is love."

"What – what about having a marriage of convenience?" She wanted to believe him. She wanted to believe him so desperately that she ached.

But for better or for worse, she was no longer the naïve girl who had blindly believed in fairy tales and happily-ever-afters. She was stronger. Braver. And she would never again settle for anything less than what she deserved.

"I don't want convenience." He laced their fingers together. "I want *you*. I want you not because of what you can give me, but because you make me happy. You bring light into my darkness, Caroline. So I want you. Just you. For the rest of my life."

"What are you doing?" She stared at him in disbelief when he dropped down to his knee and pulled the gold band she'd tried to throw into the fire out of his pocket.

"Asking you to marry me. Properly, this time." He looked up at her countenance, and whatever he saw in the swirling depths of her gray eyes made him smile. "Lady Caroline Elizabeth Wentworth, would you do me the great honor of being my wife?" He paused. "Again."

"Well at least you remembered my name this time," she said, blinking back tears.

"Is that a yes?"

"Yes." She dashed her knuckles beneath her lashes. "Yes, I do believe it is."

He gently slid the ring onto her finger and then

leapt to his feet to pull her into a hard, lingering embrace. "I love you," he said fiercely. "I love you so bloody much. And I'm going to spend the rest of my life proving it to you."

"I love you too," she said, smiling through her tears. "I love you too."

Together they lit the Yuletide log and stood wrapped in each other's arms as it caught fire and started to burn. With a contended sigh Caroline rested her head on Eric's shoulder, and he pressed his lips to her hair. It wasn't the Christmas either one of them had been expecting.

But that was what made it so perfect.

ABOUT THE AUTHOR

Jillian Eaton grew up in Maine and now resides in Pennsylvania. When she isn't writing, Jillian is doing her best to keep up with her three very mischievous dogs. She loves horses, coffee, getting email from readers, ducks, and staying up late finishing a good book.

She isn't very fond of doing laundry.

www.jillianeaton.com

AUTHOR'S NOTE

I sincerely hope you enjoyed the time you've spent with Caroline and Eric! If you liked The Winter Duchess – or even if it wasn't quite your cup of tea – please consider taking the time to leave a review. It only takes a few minutes, but every review has a huge impact, especially for an Indie Author like me!

And please continue reading for a sneak peek at A Dangerous Seduction (Bow Street Brides #1), available now in paperback!

A DANGEROUS SEDUCTION

A MURDER....

When Lady Scarlett Sherwood's husband is killed in a riding accident that turns out to be no accident at all, she becomes the number one suspect in a murder investigation that takes the ton by storm. Her accuser? None other than the dark, ruthless Sir Owen Steel, Captain of the Bow Street Runners... and the only man Scarlett has ever loved.

A BETRAYAL...

Owen was just the poor son of a baker when Scarlett spurned him for a highborn lord. Now he is one of the most powerful men in England, but he never forgot the woman who left him humiliated and heartbroken. He always vowed he would make Scarlett pay for her treacherous betrayal, and what better way to seek revenge than to see her imprisoned for murder?

A DANGEROUS SEDUCTION...

But old passions are hard to ignore, and one kiss is all it takes for Owen and Scarlett's sizzling chemistry to be reignited. Soon they find themselves swept up in an affair that could have dangerous consequences for them both. Because there is still a murderer on the loose, and he's just found his next victim...

Scarlett.

ALL OF THE COLOR DRAINED OUT OF SCARLETT'S FACE.

Owen couldn't be here.

It was impossible.

Except it wasn't. Ruth would never lie to her, especially about something so important.

"Where is he?" Her gaze flew to the door but it was partially closed, obscuring her view of the hallway. "How long has he been here? Did he request me specifically?"

"Mr. Givens admitted him into the front parlor ten minutes ago." Ruth shifted her weight from one foot to the other. "And yes, he made a point of requesting you specifically, my lady."

"Of course he did," Scarlett muttered under her breath before she drew back her shoulders. Part of her was tempted to simply send Owen away. He never should have come here in the first place. What if

Rodger had been at home? It would have been nothing short of a disaster. Yet there was no denying that she desperately wanted to see him again. How many times had she practiced what she would say if they were to ever come face to face? A thousand? Ten thousand? She'd lost track years ago.

"Tell Captain Steel…" She hesitated as she struggled to control her conflicting emotions. "Tell Captain Steel I will be with him shortly."

Ruth's eyes widened. "Are you certain that is a good idea? Perhaps you should wait until Lord Sherwood returns home. It would not be seemly for you to visit with a man when your husband is away."

The irony of Ruth's statement coaxed the tiniest of smiles from Scarlett's lips. "It is not *seemly* that my husband is out carousing with his mistress when he should be here with me." One pale brow lifted a notch. "I am entertaining an old friend, Ruth. And that is precisely what you will say should anyone ask. Do you understand?"

"Yes my lady," the maid murmured as she stepped to the side, giving Scarlett room to pass. After pinching her cheeks to bring some color back into them, she lifted her chin, murmured a quick prayer, and glided into the parlor.

Her gaze was immediately drawn to a broad set of

shoulders encased in a dark jacket. Owen – could it *really* be him? – was standing in front of the mantle with his back to the room. As if he sensed her presence those broad shoulders suddenly stiffened, his entire body coiling like a panther ready to spring as he slowly turned to face her.

"Lady Scarlett." His voice was deeper than she remembered. He was taller as well, his body lean and well-muscled, evidence of his physical prowess found in the width of his shoulders and the definition of his thighs. His hair was still just as dark, but it was a touch longer than the last time she'd seen him, curling low over his brow and brushing against the collar of his jacket. And his eyes… She caught her breath. His eyes were as cold as the sleeting rain lashing at the windows. "Or should I say Lady Sherwood now?"

"Scarlett is fine." Not trusting herself to go any closer than absolutely necessary she remained by the door, one hand curled tightly around the brass knob. Her heart was beating so fast she feared Owen would hear it, but if he did he gave no indication. His countenance was completely devoid of expression, giving away none of what he was feeling.

If he was even feeling anything at all.

Owen shrugged as if it did not matter to him one way or the other. Then his eyes narrowed as his gaze came to rest on the exposed curve of her collarbone where a blonde tendril brushed against ivory skin. "You've cut your hair."

"Yes." Self-consciously her hand drifted to where he was looking, fingers fidgeting with the edge of her bodice before she forced her arm to drop. "A few days ago. I found long hair no longer suited me."

"You were always good at getting rid of things that no longer suited you."

Scarlett drew a sharp breath. She had wondered how long it would be before he fired the first shot. The tiny barb hurt her more than she'd thought it would, drawing blood before it buried beneath her skin. "What – what are you doing here, Owen? What do you want?"

What *was* he doing in London, a place he had always despised? And why was he dressed so formally in a gray tailcoat, stark white neck cloth, and beige breeches that clung to his muscular legs like a second skin? The last time she'd seen him he had been wearing his father's hand-me-downs that were two sizes too big and worn so thin as to nearly be see-through. Now every stich of his wardrobe looked as though it had been tailor-made. If she did not know any better she would have thought him at least a baron, mayhap even a viscount or an earl.

There were other things she'd wanted to say. Other words she'd wanted to use. But the mere sight of him had washed all of those words away, leaving her with nothing but a long list of questions she desperately wanted answered.

Where have you been all these years?

Are you married?

Do you have a family?

Do you hate me for what I did?

She did not have to ask the last question. The answer was already written across every inch of his cold, formidable countenance. Yes, Owen hated her... and the worst part was she couldn't even blame him for it. Not after what she had done. To him. To them. To the future they should have had.

"I have come to inform you of your husband's passing."

He spoke so bluntly that for a moment his words and the meaning behind them did not sink in. When they did Scarlett brought both of her hands to her mouth with a gasp and reeled back against the door, her skull striking the wood with a heavy *thud*.

"What?" she managed to croak between her fingers. "Rodger is d-dead? How…"

"He fell from his horse and broke his neck," Owen stated matter-of-factly. "His body was recovered early this morning in the theatre district. Do you know why he would have been there?"

Scarlett stared at Owen with eyes awash in tears, unable to believe not only what he was saying but *how* he was saying it. For all the emotion in his voice he might as well have been talking about the dreary weather or the recent appointment of a new Speaker of the House in Parliament.

"You must be mistaken." Her own voice was shrill and filled with incredulity. Rodger was *dead*? Impossible. She'd seen him just last night in the library! What were the last words she had spoken to him? Had they been cruel? Kind? Indifferent? Suddenly it was imperative that she remember. She squeezed her eyes shut, searching the vestiges of her memory. He had insinuated she join him in his bed and she… she had asked if he still had his mistress.

His mistress who lived in the theater district.

Scarlett's eyes flew open.

"Where did you say the body was found?"

"The theater district." Owen watched her closely, studying every wayward emotion that rippled across her expressive face as she flew through the stages of shock, denial, and finally grief.

Scarlett may not have loved Rodger, but that did not mean she ever wished for him to die. Well, perhaps in a moment of anger… but this was different. This was *permanent*. Her husband was dead. And the man she'd spurned so she could marry him had delivered the news.

"*What did you do?*" Without thinking she flew at Owen with her hands raised and managed to rake her nails across the shadow of scruff clinging to his jaw before he captured her wrists and pinned them against his chest.

"Nothing," he snarled, restraining her easily as she continued to claw and kick and scratch. "I did not kill him. You are going to hurt yourself. Stop it. Scarlett, I said *stop it*."

It was the sound of her name spilling from his lips that finally pierced the thick fog of furious grief. She froze, her chest rising and falling on a gasping breath as she dragged air into her lungs. When the hazy mist rolled away she realized Owen had both of his arms banded around her body. She felt the burn of his touch through the layers of fabric that separated them, the scorching heat of it as achingly familiar as it was painful.

It *hurt* to be this close to him again.

It hurt her body.

Her mind.

Her very soul.

Peeking up at him beneath a thick sweep of blonde lashes she saw his entire jaw was rigid, his icy blue gaze pinned to the far wall. And she couldn't help but wonder if he felt it too. The burn. The heat. The *need*.

Rodger is dead, she reminded herself harshly. *Before you throw yourself into the arms of another man perhaps you'd best mourn the one you just lost.*

"You can release me now," she said stiffly. "I – I apologize. I did not mean to insinuate you had anything to do with Rodger's death."

One dark eyebrow shot up. "And here I thought that was exactly what you were insinuating." But he let her go nevertheless and she quickly stepped back, putting some much needed space between them even as she cursed her inability to control her emotions.

No matter how angry Rodger made her, she had always been able to command a façade of indifference. Whether she *choose* to do it or not had depended on how much she wanted to infuriate him, but at least she'd been able to pick whether she wanted to be angry or aloof. But with Owen she'd never been able to make that choice. No matter how hard she tried, she could not hide what she was feeling from him. It made her feel small and vulnerable; two things Scarlett was not accustomed to feeling.

Lifting her chin she met his gaze without flinching; no small feat given the erratic flutter of her pulse and the hard, rapid pounding of her heart. "If my husband really is dead–"

"He is."

"–then how is that *you* are the one to inform me?" Her glare let him know she did not like being interrupted. The faint smirk lurking in the corners of his mouth told her he did not care.

"It is my duty."

"Your duty?" Her brow creased with confusion. "What do you mean your duty?"

"I am a Runner."

He did not need to say anymore. Everyone – even Scarlett, who'd never had cause to use their services – knew of the Bow Street Runners. Founded by Henry Fielding, they were Britain's first organized police force. Comprised of a handful of highly skilled men, most of which had military backgrounds, the Runners were responsible for upholding law and order on London's busy streets and the outlying towns and villages.

Scarlett had met a Runner only once before. He'd been called to a dinner party she was attending after a guest's emerald necklace went missing. Eventually it was discovered the necklace had slipped off in the carriage and the Runner had left, leaving a swirl of excited gossip in his wake as he'd been quite handsome, but not nearly so pleasing to look at as Owen.

It was a job that suited him, Scarlett decided. He certainly had the look of a Runner: tall and long-limbed with broad shoulders and dark features. He had the mind as well. Always determined to do the right thing no matter the cost. At least now she knew what he was doing in London.

"How did it happen? How did… how did Rodger pass away?" She knew he'd already told her, but in her shock she had forgotten.

"It appears he fell from his horse and his head struck the cobblestones. I am sure you can imagine the rest."

Scarlett flinched. Yes, she could, even though she did not want to. She shook her head to clear the image of her husband sprawled lifeless on the street with his head cracked open like an egg, then knit her eyebrows together in confusion. "But that does not many any sense. Rodger is" – *was* – "an excellent equestrian." If there was one thing Rodger had always been good at, it was riding horses. To her knowledge he'd never even had a fall, let alone one serious enough to do him any harm.

"Indeed." His eyes narrowing on her face, Owen studied her with an intensity that caused blood to rush to her cheeks. "I find it rather curious myself. Did you say you knew why he would be in the Theatre District?"

"I – I have no idea." Lying about Rodger's affairs had become as second nature to Scarlett as breathing. Shifting uncomfortably beneath Owen's harsh scrutiny she walked around the back of an elegant sofa, her fingers trailing along the wooden framework. "He must have had business."

"Before dawn?" Owen watched her as a hawk watched a mouse, his penetrative gaze never leaving her slender body. Not liking his tone or his unwavering stare, Scarlett stopped in front of a large window that looked out over the side lawn.

"I am not always privy to my husband's schedule." It was still raining, the sky a gloomy, depressing gray. She watched as droplets of water trickled down the outside of the window. They pooled along the sill before spilling over and cascading across the glass in tiny streams that randomly intersected before splitting off again. *Not unlike Owen and I*, she thought with a bitter twist of her mouth. Fate – or more accurately Rodger's death – may have brought them into the same room again, but they were still very much apart.

The way Owen was speaking to her... she almost would have preferred he yelled. Anything would have been better than cold indifference, especially when it was tainted with a hint of accusation.

"Why are you asking me so many questions?" She peered at him over her right shoulder, arched brows pulled in close together. "Are you implying that my husband's death was not an accident?"

"I don't know, Lady Sherwood." His head canted to one side as he stretched his arm out and rested his hand on the edge of the mantle, fingers tapping absently against the stone. "Was it?"

"Of course it was." She did not like the way he was looking at her. Almost as if he were a predator... and she was his prey. "If Rodger fell from his horse as you claim, how could it be anything *but* an accident?"

"I am not certain." And yet he still continued to watch her, his glacial stare causing the downy hairs on the back of her neck to rise.

"Surely you do not think *I* had anything to do with it?"

"Until the investigation has been completed I cannot rule anything – or anyone – out."

Scarlett whirled to face Owen in a swirl of green muslin. "That is preposterous!"

"Is it?" he countered softly.

"*Yes*. It is no secret that Rodger likes…" She paused, her tongue twisting as she forced herself to speak in the past tense. "*Liked* to drink too much. He was probably foxed and his horse stumbled and he fell. A horrible accident, but an accident nevertheless."

Owen's hand dropped from the mantle and slid into the pocket of his breeches. "Where were you last night?"

"Here. I was here all night."

"Alone?"

"Not that it is any of your business but yes, I was."

He rubbed his chin. "Now I find that rather curious."

"Do you?" she said coolly.

"Yes. You see, I asked around a bit before I came here. If I am not mistaken, there was a ball last night. A ball you were expected to attend."

Scarlett bristled. She did not like what Owen was saying. More than that, she didn't like what he was *not* saying. "If I attended every dinner party and ball I was invited to I would never have time for anything else. Unless enjoying a quiet evening at home is a crime, I haven't done anything wrong!"

"Just asking a few routine questions, Lady

Sherwood," he drawled. "There's no need to get upset."

"I am not upset. And you do not need to call me that." Once Owen had known her better than anyone else. Even better than she knew herself. And it hurt more than she could possibly put into words to have him treat her as if she were a stranger.

"What should I call you?"

"My name."

A humorless smile lifted the corners of his mouth. "I thought I was."

Very well, she thought silently. *If that is how you want it...*

"If there is nothing else, Captain Steel, I shall have Graves escort you out."

Owen began to slowly button his coat. "Your husband's body will be delivered by the end of the day so you can begin funeral arrangements. Oh, and one more thing. You don't happen to have any green velvet hair ribbons by chance, do you?"

Scarlett blinked. "Green velvet hair ribbons? I suppose I might. I'm not entirely certain. What does that have to do with anything?"

"Simple curiosity, Lady Sherwood." He walked past her to the door. "By the way, I am sorry for your loss."

"Yes." Scarlett's smile was so brittle it was a wonder her mouth did not crack into a thousand pieces. "I am sure you are."

Printed in Great Britain
by Amazon